# Marked

## Stuart Park

# MARKED

## STUART PARK

SINISTER
HORROR
COMPANY

Marked

First Published in 2016

Cover illustration by Jorge Wiles.
Chapter page illustration by Clare Robertson.
Cover design by LikeBreathing.

ISBN-13: 978-0993592690

LikeBreathing.com

# ACKNOWLEDGEMENTS

Thanks to Clare Robertson for her proof-reading, the chapter page illustration and support.

Thanks to Willemijn Barker-Benfield for her proof-reading and feedback.

Thanks to Miho Tse for her translation advice.

Thanks to Jorge Wiles for his cover illustration.

Thanks to Justin Park for his proof-reading, support and guidance along this journey.

Thanks to my right knee for the time and inspiration to make this happen.

To my brothers who give me black and white to my grey.

"Shit happens, then you die!"
Trevor Kent

# Prologue

Stuart Park

Kim knew it was exactly twenty years since that day. That day she'd never forgive herself for.

It was Mark's idea, but she'd been just as enthusiastic agreeing; so that was settled. Times were tough back then but they needed a break, they needed to take the twins and get away, get out of the house. Those four walls felt like a prison. They wanted an escape, a change of scenery. A day out to 'Stanswick Sands' sounded like the perfect idea.

They etched themselves out a small spot on the already crowded beach. The weather was glorious for that late in the year and they were glad they'd made the most of it. Kaylyn was always more adventurous than her brother, choosing to splash around in the surf with her father. She insisted on wearing her pink dress everywhere, "To be just like mummy." Kim had to change into her bathing suit just

3

so her daughter would copy. Kaylyn's brother, Ben, stayed on the safety of dry land with his mother, making sandcastles. He'd decided the water was too cold and would rather hunt for strewn litter to make flags for his sandy fortress. He carved out doorways for invisible men to enter before crushing the stronghold with flames from the soaring *dragon*.

Kaylyn was fascinated by the seagulls, watching them swoop and dive over the shore ready to pounce on any unattended sandwich or half eaten ice cream cone. She was always giggling and on the move, meaning her parents needed to take turns so they could sit down and enjoy a rest. Ben was happy to stay put, digging holes and pointing out the ships on the horizon. He wasn't happy with either of his parent's answers to why the boats wobbled on the sea. 'Because it's hot,' simply didn't satisfy his curiosity, although he was pleased to learn the word 'shimmer'.

After a day at the seaside they packed up and decided to take the scenic route back to the car. Both Mark and Kim each had to carry one of their four-year-olds up the steps to The Lookout, but it was worth it for the views alone. From the top of the cliffs they could see right across the bay and down to the small ant-like people that scuttled around the shore. The breeze was stronger but the sun was still warm, despite it hanging low in the sky.

As the last treat of the day, Mark and Ben waited in line for a round of ice creams whilst Kim and Kaylyn wandered through the mass of people enjoying their well earnt weekends, looking for a place to sit. Kaylyn held Kim's hand as she smiled up at her mother through the same blonde hair that tumbled over both their shoulders. They agreed they'd found the perfect spot.

Kim pointed to her husband and son, encouraging Kaylyn to wave and shout, "Daddy and Ben, over here!"

The pair, still queueing, spied them through the moving heads. They returned their waves and beaming smiles.

Looking back down to her side, Kim's heart stopped. Her grin vanished.

Kaylyn had gone.

Her waving became a distress call to her husband. Frantically she span around, looking one way, then the other. She shouted for her daughter, looking to people nearby asking if they'd seen a small blonde girl.

They hadn't.

But she was just here. She couldn't have gone far.

Kim picked out every child she could see, none were her Kaylyn. Over the background noise she recognised the familiar giggle she knew so well. In the distance she could see her daughter chasing seagulls near the edge of the cliff. Screaming again, she turned to run and collided with a father carrying his son. Slightly dazed she clambered back to her feet, Kaylyn had vanished again. She rushed to the cliff's edge. Looking over, Kim could see a small child in a pink dress and golden hair sprawled on the rocks far below. Kim reached out losing her footing on the loose stone.

She felt herself fall.

There was a tight grip around her wrist as she was pulled backwards.

Kim screamed, "LET ME GO! LET ME GO!"

Finding herself back on her feet, her eyes met with Mark's. Again she screamed, pulling away from her husband, towards the precipice. Mark clutched his wife tightly as they both peered over the edge.

"What is it?" Mark implored. "Where's Kaylyn?"

Looking down to the rocks the couple could see nothing *but* rocks.

"She was there," Kim exclaimed, insisting, their daughter had fallen.

Mark firmly shook his wife, "Kim, where is Kaylyn? Where is she?"

He looked up to see Ben stood in front of the ice cream seller, the friendly vendor's hands on either side of his son's shoulders. Ben watched his parents. His mother shrieked hysterically as his father shouted at her, desperately looking in every direction.

Nervously Ben looked up and asked, "Mummy, Daddy; where's Kay?"

"Inconclusive!" screeched Kim "Inconclusive!"

"I really am very sorry," PC Phillips spoke softly to counteract Kim's anger. "You have to understand we have conflicting eye witness accounts. Even the statements from you and your husband are different."

"I saw her, I saw her on the rocks," Kim sobbed.

"But you didn't see her fall, no one did. We analysed the rocks, there were no traces of blood, hair or fibres from the clothing you mentioned."

Kim cried louder, Mark squeezed his wife's hand.

"Sorry," the PC apologised, maybe 'blood' hadn't been the best word to use in this situation. He placed his teacup back in its saucer. "If she did fall, our only conclusion is that she was carried out to sea. We sent out the helicopter team, three lifeboats and five divers. None could find any evidence. We have lifeguards further along the beach, they have all been briefed but have found nothing since."

The constable paused to let the parents absorb these facts.

"Pictures of Kaylyn have been posted around the local area, on the beach, at The Lookout and throughout the town," he took another sip of his Earl Grey. "Unless we find any evidence or anyone comes forward with more information I'm afraid there is little more we can do." The constable looked solemn.

Kim stormed from the lounge, her wailing became uncontrollable.

PC Phillips turned to Mark, "We can put you in touch with a counsellor."

"Thank you," Mark mustered as he took the card from the police man, trying to hold himself together.

He stood and showed the PC to the door.

"If we hear of anything new, we'll let you know."

They never heard from PC Phillips again.

# One

Stuart Park

*The grainy black and white images show a cityscape in some far off country. The image flicks to a flat roof at the top of a seven storey building. Dark grey blobs move around.*

*Crackling voices provide a running commentary.*

*"Four hostiles now on the roof top, three machine guns and an RPG."*

*"Weapon is being loaded, I repeat, weapon is being loaded."*

*"Lunch is served."*

*"Navigation lock green."*

*"Dispatch when clear."*

*"Confirmed, Liberation Arrow unleashed."*

*"ETA, thirty – six seconds, that's – three – six – seconds. Standby."*

*"The cheque has been signed."*

*The roof top appears closer; three figures move to the edges, the fourth arms the launcher.*

*Edges of the picture show scrolling numbers.*

"Katie."

*"ETA, seven — teen seconds, that's — one — seven — seconds. Standby."*

      *One end of the image shows:*
           *SAFETY – D/ACTV*
           *PRIMED – ACTV*
           *PAYLD – ACTV*
    *The figures circle the perimeter.*
      *"ETA, eight seconds, that's — eight — seconds."*

"Katie," repeated the voice with more intent.

    "One sec," replied Katie, not looking away from the television.

*The roof top fills the screen, the figures run towards an open door.*

    *The screen erupts into pure static. The static blinks off, cutting to a slow-motion replay of the missile striking the building from long range. The smoke and dust clear. The four moving blobs are no longer moving.*

    *"Target realised."*
    *"Analysing. 99.7% resolution."*
    *"Within operating parameters, success criteria compliance."*
    *"The bill has been paid."*

"Kate, answer your father," came a voice from the kitchen.

"Katie, what are you watching?" asked her father.

"This?" Kate pointed at the screen with a quizzical face. "It's a live stream from missile cameras."

"On the news?" he enquired.

"No, 'MissileCam' it's a dedicated channel, twenty-four-seven, live feeds from around the world."

"Why are you not getting ready for school?" her father asked.

"It's a teacher contentment day," the kitchen voice replied. "Ah yes, you can go to work with your father today."

"Mother!" Kate exclaimed in disdain.

"Actually Kim—" her father walked towards the kitchen.

Kim looked up from sorting through a basket of washing and met her husband's eyes. He halted.

"Mark," she paused, "it'll be good for her." She smiled thinly.

Mark was silent.

Kim reached for her morning coffee, and took another sip.

She continued, "Anyway, it's about time she—WHAT ARE THESE?" Kim interrupted herself, grabbing something from the washing pile and storming into the lounge. She stood between her daughter and the television holding out a pair of skinny bleached jeans.

"These are not yours, where did you get them?" Kim demanded to know.

"They were a present."

"From whom?"

"Um, no, those I borrowed from Sally," Kate stumbled.

"These wouldn't fit Sally."

"Must have been from Zara," more nervousness crept in.

"You're lying," Kim snapped back. She turned to Mark, "Have you seen these before?" Kim said, barely containing her anger.

Mark kept quiet and shrugged his shoulders, they both gave him the same evil glare.

"You stole these didn't you? You and that Chloe girl," accused her mother.

Kate's silence spoke volumes, she hid her face knowing she was beaten.

"I can't believe you're still doing this, not after last time," Kim ground her teeth. "That's it, you can go to work with your father, we will deal with this later."

Kate leapt up. "Keep taking the tablets mother," she stomped from the lounge wiping her eyes and slamming doors as she went.

"Katie, honey, you might want to change your clothes," Mark added gingerly.

He looked at his hands, "I guess she's coming with me."

"You don't mind do you Mark? It would be good for you to spend more time with her."

Mark paused and smiled, "Sure, of course." There was an uncomfortable delay as Mark struggled to maintain eye contact, although he sustained his smile, "What are you up to today?"

His wife's shoulders dropped, "Work this morning, um, I need to pick up a repeat for Zodlex, oh yeah, then therapy this afternoon. Yay me," she tried to catch her husband's gaze, but sounded too dismal, so was glad when she didn't.

"I see you're getting low on Valerian root," Mark suggested cautiously.

"I know, but I've stopped taking them, they make me dizzy."

"Maybe just cut down a little?" he was now on dangerous ground.

"Don't YOU start, you're meant to be on my—" she burst into tears.

"Okay babe, okay," Mark hugged his wife knowing he stepped over the line, she buried her face in his shoulder.

He pulled her close and watched a fuzzy, light grey building turn into a dark grey cloud of debris. Small moving blotches were being picked off by gunfire from an Apache Longbow's 30mm chain gun. The pixelated black and white figures could have been something from a cartoon. Their animated movements made the abstracted reality easier to stomach.

Kim pulled away and dried her eyes, "I dreamt of Kaylyn last night, she called to me, she said she was lost."

Mark squeezed his wife.

"You know it's been twenty years; today," she sobbed.

Mark nodded, not admitting he had also dreamt of their daughter.

"My baby still haunts me. Guess I deserve this persecution, it's all my fault," she howled with deep-seated pain as tears flooded her face.

Mark held her tight. Kim forced herself to stop, she'd cried enough over the past two decades. Her agony wouldn't let go, but for now she'd have to bury her torment for another time.

Mark released his grasp as she stepped away, wiping her face. She looked at her husband and cracked a smile, "I probably look a right state."

There was a fleeting moment of calming silence. This was broken as they both watched Kate march across the lounge.

"I'll be in the van," she growled to no one, slamming the front door.

"That's my cue. Be strong," he left his wife with a gentle peck on her forehead.

He wished he'd said something else to reassure her. Gripped her tight and promised the future would be brighter, but he didn't.

# Two

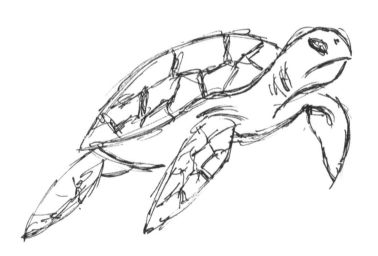

Stuart Park

Mark climbed in the van, seating himself next to the scowling face and crossed arms of his daughter. He started the engine and the radio blared through the speakers, they both jumped.

> *You might be right to save his wife, what do I see*
> *I could be wrong, where I belong*
> *Is there anything clear you stop and hear*
> *Good morning*
> *Good morn—*

Mark clicked off the music. Father and daughter looked at each other and grinned.

"So dad, where are we going anyway?"

"It's just a slash and clear job, shouldn't take all day, anyway it's not far," he sounded upbeat.

Before they reached the end of the road, Mark had pulled out a crumpled packet of cigarettes from his pocket.

"Don't tell your mother," he peered at his daughter, fighting back a smile.

"Give us one," Kate finally looked keen about something.

"I think you're in enough trouble already, don't you?"

Kate huffed and pulled out her phone.

"How's school?" he changed the subject whilst lighting his right-angled cigarette.

"Boring," Kate sunk back in her seat still playing with her phone.

"Did you see your brother this morning?" he tried again.

"Yep, I got the usual bleary-eyed-Ben frown after I offered him a coffee. I think he's on his long shift today."

The pair passed the waking world as it yawned and stretched into life.

Looking up she waved at some boy, the grin returned.

"Who's that?" Mark asked without trying to sound too nosey or fatherly.

"He's in the year above me."

"At school?"

"Yes dad, at school, where else?" the sarcasm was clearly intentional.

"Your boyfriend?"

"No."

"So, do you have a boyfriend yet?" Mark probed.

"No dad," already bored of her interrogation.

"Best way too," Mark paused, "although, a pretty girl like you, it won't be long."

Kate smiled and hoped her father wouldn't notice; he noticed.

Mark slowed to a crawl as the traffic thickened.

"You know, you should go easy on your mum, she's having a tough time at the moment," Mark tried to convey some compassion.

"She doesn't have to take it out on me all the time," his daughter bit back.

"That's just what I mean," he sighed. "Anyway, believe me, it's not just you."

"Just don't give her a reason," Mark looked across to Kate. "Please," he appealed.

She looked up, "Okay dad."

Up ahead were 'Road Closed' signs, police redirected traffic whilst orange suited men carried crates and tools from unmarked white vans to a tent erected behind the barriers. A boy walked between the cars selling small wooden animals, making use of his increased customer base in the congested traffic.

"Hey kid," Mark called out; the boy ambled over. "What's going on?" he pointed further down the road.

"First you buy one of these." The boy produced a box of wooden ornaments.

"Yeah, sure, good sales tactic." Mark chose a carved turtle, its head suspended from its body by a small piece of thread. He pulled out some loose change and a half empty packet of chewing gum from his pocket. He handed over some coins and offered both the boy and Kate some gum, they both refused, he helped himself to some.

The boy thanked him, "It's a crashed drone, I saw it hit the ground about an hour ago. The police showed up and now it's all closed off."

"Was it armed?"

The boy shrugged.

"Thanks kid." Mark shifted in his seat to find a better view of the commotion.

After several minutes of stopping and starting they reached the policeman redirecting traffic into a side street.

"What happened?" he quizzed.

"Not much sir, only a burst water main."

It felt as if the policeman had this well-rehearsed.

"Why the tent?"

"Move along sir, move along." The policeman stepped back from Mark's van waving him towards the detour.

Mark pulled away and used his freshly chewed gum to attach the turtle to the dashboard.

"You were probably watching the camera feed from that drone this morning." Mark smiled.

The turtle nodded in agreement.

"Well, this will take us a little longer. Right, since you're not at school, education time. Let me see; what's that?" he pointed.

"Oak tree," Kate responded.

"Very good, but which one?"

"A brown one," she was already losing interest.

"That's the Pedunculate Oak," he stated as enthusiastically as possible.

"Okay, what's that?" an attempt to keep this going.

Without looking up, "Grass." Kate was done.

"That's a Wych Elm sapling," now playing on his own. "There's a Monkey Puzzle Tree, but you know that," he spoke to his inattentive audience. "Ah, a bunch of sneezeweeds," private joke.

Kate's gaze drifted from her lap, but still ignoring her father; the area was becoming more built up and busier.

They passed an establishment named 'Tits & Trumpets'.

Kate laughed, "Dad, what's that place?"

"Um, not sure," lied Mark.

Her phone pinged, she looked back down and continued to tap.

"Look, there's a clump of Little Carlow," Mark instructed his non-existent listeners. "A gang of Monk's hood and a crowd of Monica Lynden-Bell."

Still playing with her phone, Katie switched the radio back on hoping it might distract her father.

> "… *sister planet is approaching its closest point for almost 3,000 years. That's right, Venus, the planet the Romans deemed the goddess of love,*

23

*beauty and fertility will be at its closest proximity to Earth later this evening.*

*Stargazers are preparing for this marvel saying it's a once in a lifetime event, last witnessed by King Solomon and the early Indian astronomers. The European Space Agency has made a statement saying this will not impact life on Earth but to simply sit back and enjoy the astrological show. Pressure groups have called for action stating the retrograde rotation, meaning the opposite to the Earth's, will slow our spin and may even change our orbit around the Sun. This would cause the continental plates to shift creating earthquakes, tidal waves and tsunamis across the globe. Emergency services have been alerted and are on stand-by for any problems this cosmic event may cause."*

# Three

Stuart Park

"Same time tomorrow," winked Oliver as he packed away his clubs.

"Of course," responded his caddy. "New wheels?"

"Had her dropped off this morning," Oliver grinned wiping off specks of dust.

"Nice colour."

Oliver nodded climbing into his pre-heated leather seats. His phoned chirped at him, the incoming number could mean only one thing. "Moth Berry," he answered.

"Hello Oliver, had a busy week?" Came a blank voice.

"According to my accountant I have," he smiled.

"Tell me Oliver, if one man takes your car would you call that stealing?"

"Yes," he replied, "and if all the men take my car, we call that democracy."

"So Oliver, how many men does it take to change the act from being unlawful to lawful?"

"In my eyes it wouldn't matter, I'd have them all horsewhipped and branded," he played along. "On more practical matters, I lost several thousand last night at the casino. Cats are never lucky for me. Then a healthy tip for the girls in H&H."

"Thank you Oliver, much appreciated."

"Anyway, something tells me this is not a social call," he quizzed.

"Your welfare is always my concern, although you are correct." The voice conveyed no emotion.

There was a pause.

"We have *acquired* Mr Barrington and I would very much like you to meet with him and oversee the unresolved affairs."

Oliver's eyes widened, "Understood. That certainly *is* news."

"Let's say, two hours. By the way, how's the new car?" The voice asked with no interest.

"How did you—" Oliver stopped himself, there was really no point in asking.

"In the morning the sun rises, in the evening the sun sets," came the explanation.

Oliver expected nothing less.

"… I know I've changed the tyres, but it's still the same car," chatted Oliver whilst rolling along a white gravel driveway. "I'm here, I'll call you back."

He stopped outside a set of marble steps. Taking a deep breath, he looked around the overgrown lawns and low hanging trees. Only the gentle trickle from the blue granite fountain tickled his ears.

"Knock, knock," Oliver called out, pushing aside the half opened door.

He followed a trail of devastation leading to the main dining room. A man was lying face down on the table, his limbs tied to each wooden leg; muffled sounds were coming from his gagged mouth. He looked up at Oliver. Oliver crouched so their eyes were level.

"Hello Oscar," he smirked, "No, no, please don't get up."

Oscar strained at his bonds.

Oliver continued, "We didn't think you were coming home, lucky for us you did. The question is, why are you back?"

"This," a teenage girl, oriental in appearance, entered the room holding a key. "Hello Mr Bexley."

She placed the key into Oliver's palm, "Ah, thank you Miho, and what does this open?"

"It fits a lock under the Corvette in the basement garage," she said matter-of-factly.

"How did you discover that?" Oliver quizzed.

She pointed at two of Oscar's fingers protruding at unnatural angles.

"We'll explore this later. First to business," Oliver turned to their hostage. "Ah, Mr Barrington, we don't like it when people fail to deliver on their promises. I'd call that rude. Lovely Miho here will show you the error of your ways," he said casually.

"What's on the menu today Miho?"

"Reiki," answered the girl.

"Ah yes, tell me Oscar, have you ever *experienced* reiki?"

The man nodded.

"I see, sophisticated. Well this is reiki with a twist, excuse the pun. I call it 'reverse reiki'. Miho will contort your muscles into the most excruciating knots. Loop over loop over loop of muscle fibre woven tight with your own tendons," explained Oliver in great delight.

Oscar's muffles increased.

"It will take you a day to even move, after that you'll barely be able to stand, let alone take a step. It will be almost impossible to clench your fingers or use your arms. You'd better find someone to feed and clean you. Then again I doubt anyone else knows you're here, except us. Don't try and seek help from a masseur," he added. "Without knowing the pattern they'll only make it worse; like pulling at your own noose. Once you've fulfilled your transaction, we'll come back and fix you; we're not monsters you know. Of course, I'm also disappointed you missed some of our sessions, sorry, but your deposit is non-refundable."

Miho prepared the room. She etched an elaborate grid into the polished ebony floor with a kitchen knife. At each intersection she placed a series of crystals. Miho explained that Carnelian and Blue Lace Agate opposite each other disrupts the subject's qi, as does Clear Quartz and Green Apophyllite. She placed a Tiger Eye gem around Oscar's neck, explaining this intensifies visions and nightmares. Then to heighten the flow, Herkimer Diamonds are scattered between the other minerals, the more impure these are, the better. To add the finishing touches, dead plants were dragged from the patio and lined the edges of the room. Then mirrors were placed at either end of their captive to create an endless feedback loop.

"I'm afraid we want to make an example of you, you understand of course. Miho will start by damaging some of your nociceptors across your shoulders and down your spine. Unfortunately for you this will magnify sensitivity to any pain. I'm really not sure if this bit is reversible, sorry about that."

Miho gripped at her victim's shirt and drew her knife across the cotton. With measured patience and an air of anticipation she cut through his clothes, removing his shirt and jacket. Once his pale torso was exposed she started her work. Oliver dusted off a chair and placed it in amongst the lifeless foliage for a ringside view.

After a few minutes Oscar began to grunt and groan interspersed with the occasional yelp. Searching his pockets, Oliver retrieved some well-worn ear plugs, and put them to use.

As time passed, Oscar's muted screams intensified. Red veins bulged in his eyeballs as sweat dripped from his forehead.

Oliver's phone vibrated.

"Moth Berry," he answered.

"Hello Oliver, how are proceedings?"

Holding out his phone Oliver signalled to Miho to remove the gag. Oscar's shrill cries echoed throughout the house.

"He's being *treated*," Oliver said simply.

"I hear. Please put me on speaker."

"Miho, please give us a moment," asked Oliver.

She stepped back and gave a small bow.

"Hello Mr Barrington, I'm feeling in a sunny disposition today, I've decided to allow you five days to conclude what's necessary," said the deadpan voice.

Oscar breathed heavily, finding it a strain to talk, "No, no, three days, no, two days, I only need two days."

The voice sounded unmoved by this plea, "Thank you for your kind offer but I feel five days is perfectly adequate. Please thank me for my generosity, otherwise it will be eight days."

"Okay, okay, tha—" his back spasmed and eyes watered, "—nk you."

"Please continue Miho."

She replaced the gag and resumed her craft. Oliver returned to his chair.

"Any thoughts as to what's in Oscar's cache?" continued the caller.

"I believe it's what we're here for," Oliver puzzled.

"Knowing Oscar, I believe it's something much more, something he's prepared to suffer for." The tone was still indifferent.

The suppressed screams continued.

"Tell me Oliver. You see two objects floating in space, from where you're observing, the gap between them grows. It appears as if one of them is moving, or are they both moving? How would you know?"

Stuart Park

# Four

Stuart Park

Mark pulled into an alleyway in the heart of the Japanese quarter. Hanro was the most vibrant and colourful place in the city, its sights, sounds and smells were an assault on the senses. It was nonstop, an insomniacs dream, or nightmare.

"Katie, put that phone down and come on," her dad insisted.

Mark climbed from the van and wandered back to the road. Dodging a bike and taking in a deep breath of raw fish he checked his scribbled notes. "Yep, this is the place, 'Kiyoshi Kampo'."

Amongst the hustle and bustle of the street was a group of three teenage girls dressed in skin-tight, pure white leather, their faces equally as white. In contrast, their hair was jet black and a pure red kiss where their lips should be were their only prominent features.

Entering the shop Mark almost collided with another of these girls. As they passed, his grey eyes locked with her piercing stare, those green orbs in her featureless face. Before their gaze broke her crimson mouth burst into a grin, revealing the same red on her lips was also smeared across her teeth.

The girls called to their friend, "Let's go Kiko."

Kate followed her father into the shop, their entrance was announced by the tinkling of tiny bells. They made their way through sacks of richly coloured spices and wooden shelves holding glass jars filled with crushed leaves and dried berries. The whole shop tasted of ginger and jasmine, a welcome relief to the old tuna he'd endured only moments ago. The shopkeeper appeared from the back, emerging through strings of bamboo.

"You must be Mr Kiyoshi," Mark enquired, reaching out his hand.

Mr Kiyoshi grinned a toothy smile and bowed.

Realising his hand had been ignored he returned it uncomfortably to his side and attempted to dip his head towards the old gentleman, not sure if this was expected, but he went through the motions anyway.

"I'm Mark, the gardener. This is my lovely assistant for today, Katie," he pointed to his reluctant daughter who gave the limpest of waves.

"Yes, yes, good, good," muttered the old man stroking his long, grey beard. He beckoned them into the back.

"How old is he?" Kate sneered.

"You know, he can hear you," Mark replied sternly.

Through the bamboo curtain lay a room lit with candles, large scorched pots slowly boiled on a stove, steam bellowed, engulfing the yellowed ceiling. Leather bound books were propped upon a large wooden table covered in sorted piles of orange granules and green flakes. The pages of the book matched the hue of the ceiling, mysterious symbols of faded ink etched into their fibre many eons ago, now barely legible.

The room led to an open air garden surrounded by the backs of other neighbouring shops and restaurants. From this side all the buildings were painted white with black water pipes and cables hanging towards the earth. A stark contrast from the multi-coloured street fronts with flowing streamers and buzzing neon lights.

The garden was compact, thick with vines, bushes and tall grasses. Walking around the small plot revealed a highly cultivated area full of immaculate rows of shrubs and herbs. Mark recognised fennel and wild ginger but nothing else. As he approached to take a closer look the old man stopped him.

Pointing to his manicured patch, Mr Kiyoshi urged, "You no go, you stay away."

"Okay, whatever you say, you're the boss," Mark shrugged.

Kate toyed with her phone, looking suitably unimpressed.

To the side of the herbs were a number of stone totems adorned with dried flowers arranged in a myriad of patterns. Symbols were engraved into the weathered granite. Surrounding the garden was a dense forest of bamboo.

Mark turned to the old man, "So what's the job exactly?"

The Japanese man pointed to the back of his shop. Stretching three stories high was a mass of Common Ivy.

"Ah, our old enemy Hedera Helix," Mark stated proudly, his knowledge falling on uneducated or uncaring ears.

Mr Kiyoshi's finger traced from the third storey down to ground-level. In front of the ivy stood bramble bushes and nettles. His finger now circled the weeds, "You clear all."

"Urtica Dioica, wow," Mark exclaimed, "the Bottle Inn would be proud of those specimens, maybe I could get some practise for the championships," he laughed to himself. "And the Rubus Fruticosus are sure getting plump," Mark was getting carried away with himself. "Um, clear the whole lot you say," Mark looked for some recognition and assurance.

The Japanese man smiled, bowed and disappeared back into his shop. Mark took that as a *yes*.

A wooden gate from the garden led into the alleyway making access easy, Mark saw his van at the other end.

"Hey honey, work time," sung Mark to his daughter.

"I am not getting up there," Kate remarked, pointing to the top window.

"Don't worry, just help me with these ladders."

As the afternoon drew on Mark realised how invasive the ivy had become. At points it seemed to disappear into the weathered brickwork under the white exterior.

Two wasps' nests later and Mark was down to the first storey. He looked out across the garden and saw Kate milling around idly in the herb plot.

Mark called out to his daughter, "Hey Katie, stay out of there."

Her dad's shout made Kate jump and she dropped her phone.

"What!" Kate wailed back. "Look what you made me do."

"Come on honey, you shouldn't be in there."

Kate reached for her phone amongst the vegetation and pricked her palm on the thorns of a jet black shrub. She squealed in pain squeezing her hand.

"Be careful," her dad called out, descending the ladder.

"It's bleeding," Kate sobbed.

"Let me see," Mark took her hand, examining the puncture wound.

"It's only a scratch, there are some plasters in the van," he added calmly.

Kate screamed, "I'm bored of this shit," and stormed through the gate up the alleyway.

"Okay honey, stay in the van, I'm almost finished."

Mark tidied the last of the clippings, packed his tools and passed through the kitchen. The pans were still bubbling, this time giving off a thick brown smoke. Mark coughed on the vapour and made his way to the shop front. Mr Kiyoshi was chatting to a Japanese man in his early twenties with bleached blonde hair and eyebrows. As the gardener entered, their talking stopped. They bowed towards each other and the young man left clutching a brown paper package.

Feeling pleased with himself, "I'm all done, I even got rid of those wasps nests, although they didn't go without a fight." He scratched several bumps on the back of his hand to prove a point.

"The sting, that no good?" the old man said worriedly, searching his selves.

"No, that's fine," replied Mark. "Hardly my first encounter with wasps, just an occupational hazard."

"They no wasps," the shopkeeper motioned to the amber looking swellings on Mark's hand.

"Nah, I'll be fine and dandy," shrugged Mark, "just payment and I'll be off."

The old man stroked his wispy beard, opened his antique cash register and began counting out Japanese Yen.

"No, no, sorry, real money," interrupted Mark, smiling.

The old man thought for a moment, his face widened, pointing to his shelves, "You take."

"No, sorry, not my thing, I have no idea what most of this is anyway."

He thought again and turned to Mark. "You take me daughter, you see her before," he made gyrating motions with his hips.

"What, no, come on," Mark disbelieving what he heard, "I'm old enough to be her father."

"She …" he held up two fingers, then four fingers.

"Twenty-four huh, same age as Ben," he pondered. "Where is your wife?" Mark questioned.

"You want wife?" he revolved his groin again.

"No, no, can I speak to her?"

"Wife …" Mr Kiyoshi motioned upwards with a pointed finger. At this he started to sob.

Mark heard a jingle from behind him and turned to see an old Japanese lady shuffle into the shop. She stared at Mark with disgust.

"You do this?" she pointed towards the elderly shopkeeper. The old lady waved her arms and started to shout at Mark, attracting other fellow supporters to enter and join the woman in her protest for him to leave. After several minutes of Mark failing to make his claims of innocence heard over the clamour he knew this was one battle he couldn't win. A beaten Mark made his retreat towards the front door and left the unruly mob behind. The jingle of the door signalled his exit.

# Five

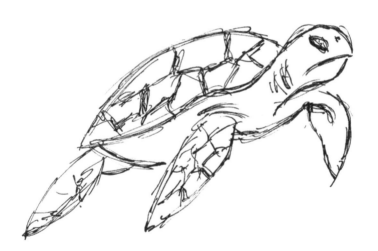

Stuart Park

Today every four-year-old was Kaylyn.

Kim checked her face in her makeup mirror, nothing a bit of blusher wouldn't conceal. There, all good to go. She strode into the office as if it were any other day.

She threw a keen, "Morning Pam!" to her assistant and collected a pile of résumés from her 'in' tray. Without any hesitation Kim split the stack and dropped the bottom handful into her assistant's rubbish bin.

"Morn— why are you thro—" Pam wasn't sure which sentence to finish.

"It eliminates the unlucky candidates," Kim interrupted her without making eye contact.

Even before she opened her office door she could smell the dense earthy aroma of the Americano waiting on her desk.

A smile swept across her face as she called out, "Thank you Pam!"

After spending most of the morning reading through fabricated qualifications and over inflated egos she stretched her legs and gazed from the window. Her thoughts drifted from CVs to Kate to twenty years ago to, *what next?*

She snapped back into reality as her phone rang.

"Your eleven o'clock is here, a Mr Parsons," confirmed her assistant.

"Thanks Pam, make him wait fifteen minutes, then send him in."

What next? No idea.

Kim had picked out one particular résumé as a definite potential and jotted down a series of notes for later.

"Yes," she called out to the knock at her door, inviting in that familiar taste.

Her assistant led in Mr Parsons. More importantly, she placed a warming bitter brew on Kim's desk, replacing the previous cup. The man pointed towards the steaming coffee, but was unsuccessful in catching Pam's attention.

Kim was still making notes. She shouted out, "Thank you," as the door clicked shut. Finally looking up at the man, Kim attempted a smile. "You must be …" she looked down at her notes, "Kipp Parsons."

"Please call me KP," he acknowledged eagerly.

"You do know why you're here?" she quizzed.

Kipp nodded.

"So Kipp, let me understand this correctly, you're writing your biography in the office during work hours. This is clearly *not* the job we pay you for," Kim stated.

"No, no, no, I've written my autobiography, now I'm reading it," responded Kipp.

"So you're reading about everything you've done until now, like a diary."

"No, I'm reading about the things I'll do in the future, then doing them."

Kim paused, tracing his facial expressions for any inkling of sarcasm; there was none.

"So, you've written down your whole life and now you're acting it out?"

"That's the idea," Kipp was pleased someone was taking an interest.

Kim stopped herself and counted down from five, taking a deep breath and a sip of coffee, "So how's your life going? Is it on track?"

"Um, so-so I guess."

"Could one buy this book?"

"Sure it's available online, I'll send you—" Kim raised her hand glaring at him.

"Does it say you'll get fired from this job?" she was losing interest.

"I'm not sure," he shrugged.

Kim looked up and paused, expecting more, none came.

"If you've written it, how do you *not* know what it says?" Kim was clearly annoyed. "Actually, please don't answer that," she sighed, "I've made a note that we've had this conversation. Memory Inc. does not abide by this behaviour, if it happens again you'll receive a written warning. Three warnings is an automatic dismissal. You may leave," she chanted, without bothering to make eye contact, then returned to her drink.

"Yellow Berry," declared Kim as she answered her phone.

"Hello Kimberley," said the impersonal voice.

"To what do I owe this pleasure?" Kim smiled.

"I know what today is, but how are you fixed for this afternoon?"

Kim checked, "Nothing that can't wait."

"I need you on the sixth, say two hours, I'll send you the details."

"Sure," she replied, opening the file she had promptly received, "also, I have something for you."

"Please continue," there was almost intrigue in the caller's voice.

"I have a CV from a Mr Lucas Green that you might be interested in. He's applying for the Cyber Security Consultant role, monitoring for network breaches; specialising in access control, vulnerabilities, exploits, firewalls, encryption, risks, threats, and so it goes on. There are gaps in his employment history and he's worked for most of our competitors. Background checks show a military history, three years as a Communications Officer, then five years as a Bomb Disposal Expert. Criminal record shows a few scuffles with the law as a teenager but nothing serious. His address is a PO Box number."

"Is he underplaying it? Something he's not telling us by leaving holes in his CV?"

"Those were my thoughts," she agreed.

"Thank you Kimberly, send me the details, we'll speak later," the voice was still expressionless.

"I'm expected," Kim said firmly to the receptionist.

"One moment please," she was instructed in return.

Stepping towards the window, Kim's heals echoed around the cavernous room. She peered down at the ground below and wondered what it would be like for those brief seconds amongst the gulls, hearing nothing but that rushing sound. Would there be peace?

"You can go through," the receptionist signalled towards a door that buzzed open.

Kim was led down a dark wood panelled corridor and into a windowless room. A number of tables were arranged in a large square. She sat in the only chair available near the entrance. Hot vapour breached her senses from the rich pungent cup of Café Cubano that waited for her. On the other side of the square sat a relaxed man with sharp features in a ruffled shirt. To her right was a large mirror spanning the length of the wall. To her left was a small stern looking oriental girl clad in white. After a brief glance towards the girl, her focus returned to the man.

"I'm—" Kim started.

The man interrupted, "I know exactly who you are, you're the MILF they summoned from downstairs, I know all about you. You should be more careful."

She waited to make sure he'd finished. He seldom blinked and was noticeably comfortable with direct eye contact.

"Fine," Kim sighed. "For the purposes of this dialogue you will be known as 'Canning'."

"Not 'Barking' then," he laughed.

"I caught the glance of a crow this morning on my way here, did you?" Kim questioned.

"Is this a test?" Canning asked.

"Everything's a test," she mocked.

Kim paused.

"If I caught a glance of that crow I wouldn't be here," he answered finally.

"Why, superstitious?"

"No, fate. It would have led me down a different path, that's all."

Kim reeled off a list of prescribed questions, adapting them to fit her subject.

"If I said 'buinasu, aishiteru', what would you say?"

"Do you really?" he snapped.

"Can you remember a day where you didn't look at the time?"

"Holbox Island. Although I spin my own cycles."

"How would you disarm a nuclear bomb?"

"Carefully," Canning laughed.

"Why does everything change?"

"Yesterday it was raining, today it's bright."

"If you could kill one person and get away with it, who would it be?"

"You."

"What one question would you ask God?"

"I'd ask, 'what question should I ask you?'."

"God would say, 'if you're asking a question you must think there's a problem'."

"So there's my answer," he said smugly.

"What part of the brain controls breathing and other involuntary actions?"

"Medulla oblongata."

"How wrong do you think you are?"

"If I knew I was wrong, I'd be right," Canning seemed very sure of himself and began to lose interest in this game.

"Should the bombing continue?"

"So long as there is a purpose."

"If the purpose was to flex military muscle?"

"Then yes, it should."

"To reduce the population?"

"Then yes."

"To instil fear and strengthen control?"

"Of course".

"When should it stop?"

"When there is no longer a reason."

"Will there ever *not* be a reason?"

"So long as someone has something to gain there will always be a reason," his eyes drifted around the room.

"Can you remember a time before you were born?"

"For breakfast I had eggs."

"Why eggs?"

"Cluck-cluck," he watched a harlequin dragon weave through the shadows avoiding the light.

"If I said you could fuck me how would you do it?"

Canning paused, the dragon disappeared into the murk, his gaze snapped back to Kim as he slowly leant forward and cracked a smile, "I think you know."

Kim broke his stare and looked down to her cup; she knew.

"What is C11 H17 N3 O8?"

"Oh, nasty! Although I prefer Botulinum, used in Botox, but I'm sure you know that."

"Everything in the world survives by eating something else."

Canning licked the tip of each finger on his left hand and smacked his lips in delight.

"What happened in Basra?" Kim played her joker.

"How— Nothing, that's what happened in Basra."

Kim paused, the room was silent.

Canning began to look agitated, this time Kim's unflinching stare burrowed into his face. After what could have been a lifetime of stillness Canning revealed a lengthy knife.

The game was over.

"You really want to know? I'll show you the *nothing* that happened," he threatened.

The Japanese girl who had been motionless for the entire time, raised from her seat and slowly moved towards the intimidator. Canning turned and swung at the girl. She grasped his knife hand, her other hand clasped his hair and pulled his head towards the table with a solid thud. With his head laying on the polished wood the girl pushed the blade through both his cheeks, pinning his head firmly to the glossy surface. She turned and sauntered back to her chair, leaving the immobilised man still clutching the hilt of his own knife.

"How did he get that thing in here?" Kim's gaze ambled from the girl, who simply shrugged, to the large mirror on her right.

Kim rested her head on the table, mirroring Canning's, "I think we're done here, don't you?"

On the walk back to reception Kim's phone vibrated.

"Yellow Berry."

"Analysis please," asked the stony voice.

"VKD above average, he's 92% ESTP. Given the right motivation he could fulfil your requirements. Although needs some work on the physical, oh and some stitches," listed Kim.

"Thank you Kimberley, as always. By the way, how would he fuck you?" The voice was still blank.

"The man is a psychopath, he'd use one of my eye sockets."

# Six

Stuart Park

Mark headed back to the alley keeping an eye on the shop door, no one followed him outside. Checking the van he realised his daughter was not there. No note, nothing.

"Ah, kids," he mumbled. Pulling out his phone he had no messages or missed calls. Kate's number went straight to voicemail. "Hi honey, this is dad, um, I've finished for the day, give me a call when you get this, love you."

Phoning home was met with equally no response.

Becoming more worried, Mark scanned the local area trying to decide in which direction to start searching.

"Where would she go? What would she do?" he thought out loud whilst rubbing his five o'clock shadow. Even though she's a teenager, Mark still had that sinking feeling in his stomach and fought back old but familiar memories; he refused to even think the worst.

Dusk settled over the city, giving Hanro an orange glow.

Weighing up his options Mark took a soothing breath and headed deeper into the confusion. The next street was teeming with market vendors packing up for the day, he knew this was not a good idea, but had to start somewhere. He pulled out his phone and flicked through to a snap of his daughter in a wetsuit carrying a surfboard. He smiled remembering their holiday last year in Les Cavaliers, a happier time.

Plunging into the mass of chatter and motion he started at a stall with towers of stacked limes and peaches.

Stopping a teenage boy carrying a crate of luminous blue berries he enquired, "Have you seen this girl?"

The boy looked at the picture and shook his head. Mark carried on through the throng being knocked and pushed. He asked at a stall selling bottles of Karone and Jaroni, having to shout just to be heard. This was met by the familiar head shaking. Packets of 'Amber Maiden' lined glass-fronted cases stacked behind the alcohol. He continued on past raw fish and giant crabs, almost slipping on a piece of forgotten skate. Then on to grey and black computer chips that were pressed into anti-static foam, all ordered by make, model and part number.

Most traders didn't even acknowledge Mark, too eager to bundle their wares and leave for the day. Dodging trays of clay and wooden pipes and an entire stall of moulded plastic goods where everything was red, he became surrounded by rolls of silk and cotton. A middle aged woman took his hand and sat him down offering him a bowl of steaming tea. Mark smiled and thanked her.

The Japanese woman laughed, "You lost, huh?"

Sipping his tea Mark revealed his phone, he sighed, "I'm looking for my daughter, have you seen her?"

"Good tea, huh?"

Mark nodded in agreement.

"Let me think," the lady added, tapping her temple. Looking at Mark she plucked a battered cloth tape-measure from her pocket. Stretching out Mark's arm she ran the tape from his armpit to his wrist. "New suit might help, huh?"

Placing down his half-finished bowl of tea he stood up to leave, "Um, maybe, but not today."

The woman called out, "Look for Venus," as she pointed, indicating around the next corner.

The adjoining street opened up into a square, the edges were lined with noodle and sake bars. Laughing diners slurped their stewed pork soba and shrimp ramen under neon lights. Mark approached the centre of the square where a group of workmen were making finishing touches to a wooden structure. Perched at the top was a glowing white orb, its pulsating light illuminated the onlookers, bringing their faces into stark contrast before fading to evening grey. Written across the structure was 'Buinasu, Aishiteru', the same phrase was also printed on flags and streamers that adorned the area. A nearby woman noticed the awe on Mark's face as he gaped at the elaborate construction.

"Venus," remarked the woman, "also Venus," she laughed, pointing into the sky.

The structure was surrounded by a number of cross-legged worshipers balanced on small mats, deep in meditation. Behind them a group dressed in brightly coloured clothing were lighting and releasing pure-white sky lanterns. Mark watched as they drifted high above into the twilight, the breeze swept them into the heavens, creating new constellations.

He approached a group of people shouting and pointing. On the ground was a man clutching his face, blood seeped between his fingers and formed a puddle on the stone street. One woman leered at the picture on Mark's phone he was holding and started to yell at him. He saw she was scrutinising the image.

"You've seen her?" said Mark anxiously, holding up his phone.

"She did this," the woman shrieked, before uttering words he could not understand; which was probably for the best.

"Where is she?" Mark surveyed the surrounding faces.

The woman pointed to a side street heading away from the square. She disappeared from view as the throbbing makeshift Venus darkened.

Mark rushed towards the direction she had indicated, navigating the traffic whilst traversing the busy road.

As he entered the side street he was met by the squawk of runaway chickens, followed by a group of hollering men waving cleavers and cages.

Mark jumped back to avoid the mass of clucking and sharpened steel. Without realising he stepped into the road amongst the traffic, turning to avoid a cyclist he was knocked down by a motorised rickshaw.

His head hit the ground; in a daze he tried to gather himself. The rickshaw driver leapt from his vehicle and pulled an unsteady Mark to his feet. Amid the confusion and over the ringing in his skull he heard the driver repeating, "Sorry, very, very sorry."

Mark was lifted from the road and bundled into the rickshaw; he felt the motion of the carriage as it picked up speed. He tried to reach for his helper but couldn't focus, his hands simply flailed in empty space. Blurred lights hurtled past, the clamour of the street faded away as Mark sunk back in his seat. Venus blackened for the last time, he never saw it reawaken.

Stuart Park

# Seven

Stuart Park

She cupped his balls as she ran the tip of her tongue along the underside of his already erect penis. She knew this would make him swell to the point of bursting. She tracked her tongue around the ridge of his cock and watched the head pulsate, whilst reaching for a discarded stocking. In a single unbroken motion Kim tied one end around the base of his rock hard member. Pulling him forward to his knees she glided past him and tied the other end to the sofa leg behind him. She crawled back to the rug, giving him another lick on the way past. Slowly she spread her legs and exposed her swollen vagina, urging Oliver to enter her. He clambered forwards until he straddled Kim, the stocking stretched until it became taut. She used the end of his penis to stimulate her clitoris, moving it in small circles over her slippery nub, purring with delight.

Oliver watched Kim guide him inside her moist pussy, he slowly thrusted until she was full, his cock strained against the nylon. He caressed the curves of her body with his hands, tracing the mounds of her breasts, before slowly returning back to her hips. Her heartrate increased as Oliver intensified his momentum. Kim gradually shuffled backwards, forcing Oliver to push even harder against the fabric. His shaft filled with blood making him stiffer than before, but the stocking, acting as tourniquet prevented him from coming.

She wrapped her legs around his waist and pulled him towards her, whispering, "Harder." Oliver obeyed, wanting her more than ever. He felt her convulse and her back arch as she moaned with pleasure. He gripped her hair in one hand and tugged her head to one side, Kim squealed with desire, digging her nails into his shoulders. Beads of sweat formed on Oliver's brow, he could feel himself building despite his restraint.

Looking him in the eye Kim whispered again, "Harder, fuck me harder." The pressure was now too much, even for Kim's knot. With one final thrust Oliver erupted into Kim, gritting his teeth as his entire body spasmed in ecstasy.

Oliver laid motionless, apart from his galloping heart and humble whimpers of euphoria. Trickles of blood ran down his back, Kim drew small circles with her fingertips, licking the ends of her red digits. Lifting herself she looked down at Oliver, he turned his head and watched her bare feet glide across his floor. She wandered over to a nearby cabinet; selecting a Waterfront crystal glass she dropped in two ice cubes and poured herself a healthy measure of Bowmorne Scotch. Still naked she sunk into Oliver's desk chair and sipped the amber liquid, watching him sprawled on the rug.

Finishing her drink she called over, "Um, Oliver can I have my stocking back when you're quite finished?"

Oliver mustered the strength and pulled himself onto the sofa. Kim passed him a drink which he gladly accepted. He took a swig, sat back and watched Kim's perfect form collect her clothes from where they were abandoned.

"So now it's your turn on the couch," commented Kim, rolling up her stockings.

"It's about time," replied Oliver, pulling on his white shirt. He felt a sting, looking at his shoulder he noticed his once white shirt was now partly crimson.

Kim laughed to herself, "That's going to clash with your teal suit. I guess the fact your wardrobe and new A5 match is *no* accident."

"Don't you like my new threads, or car?" Oliver stated proudly.

Kim remained silent.

"What's up?" he enquired.

"I argued with Kate again this morning," mentioned Kim matter-of-factly.

"What was it this time?" questioned Oliver.

"She'd been shoplifting, again." There was frustration in Kim's voice.

"And you interrogated her until she confessed."

"She was guilty, we both knew it."

Oliver paused. "You should go easy on her, it's only a phase," he said sympathetically.

"So NOW you think I shouldn't discipline my own child for committing a crime?" Kim was annoyed.

"Getting caught might be the best thing to snap her out of it," appealed Oliver.

"Is *this* therapy?" scoffed Kim.

There was an uncomfortable silence.

"She hates me," Kim continued.

"That's because you wanted her to be Kaylyn, but she's not. She will never be a substitute for Kaylyn. *Tiny Kim* has gone and she's not coming back, you know this. Kate is her own person, treat her like it."

"We've been over this, how many times now?" Kim asked rhetorically. "But where do I go from here? I've mourned and grieved to extremes. I've tried anti-depressants, moving house, religious awakening, burning her things, binge drinking, support groups, drugs, and three months on a beach in Goa. I made Mark give up his well-paid job as it reminded me of her. We buried her, but it was a hollow gesture, I knew the coffin was empty. I couldn't take solace from that."

"That should have put her to rest, spiritually," Oliver tried to find somewhere they'd not previously explored.

"Yes, but it wasn't enough. It never is," Kim sounded desperate.

"But you've never moved on from the anger stage."

"I am my anger, this is what I've become; it's now part of my very being," Kim felt her rage beginning to bubble.

"Your focus has always been either destructive or denial, you've never accepted it."

"How can I accept it when it's my fault. It's all my fault she's not here right now. Oh baby," sobbed Kim as she thought back to Kaylyn's bright eyes and cheeky smile.

"We need to find you a way out of the harmful behaviour," pleaded Oliver.

"Ha, by *harmful behaviour* you mean suicide attempts. Just say it," Kim scorned.

"But this is all well-trodden ground. No one cared, they just want it over with." Kim was feeling sorry for herself.

"I saved you from all those suicide attempts, I was there for you Kim; Mark wasn't even aware some of them ever happened," Oliver tried to stop her from following this familiar path.

"You saved me, is that all you have? You saved me, is that your complete hold over me? Well maybe you shouldn't have, maybe you should have let me fall, maybe I should have bled to death; maybe that's the answer," she was gunning for a fight. "You and all this is bullshit, pure bullshit. You can't bring back my Kaylyn. You're a constant reminder of those days, and those days are gone. All of this wallowing in self-pity, it's been too long, I have to move on," she continued her onslaught. "This has to end." Kim delivered her killer blow.

"What do you mean?" Oliver was stunned.

"I have to stop seeing you."

"But you can't. Don't do this Kim, I need this, I need you," Oliver pleaded.

"That's it Oliver. It's over. You're still a link to the past, you're a link to her."

"You can't do this," he was lost, seeking options for Kim to rescind her decision.

"I think I just have. *This* is therapy," Kim was gleefully vicious.

"Just like that, after everything, after all these years?" Oliver was still grasping.

"I needed this at the time, but not anymore, now this is just wrong, now this has to go." Oliver could feel Kim's resentment filling the room.

"I won't let it happen. I still have those pictures from a few years ago," with desperation Oliver was now forced to play his joker.

"Why, you worthless piece of shit, how dare you threaten me," Oliver's remark provoked Kim's temper to a new level.

"I—"

"So now you're blackmailing me into fucking you once a week," she fumed as her hatred boiled over.

"I—"

"You've certainly reached a new low, even for you, you self-absorbed, egotistical sorry excuse for a man," Kim's disgust made Oliver sink further back in his chair.

"Ki—"

She stepped towards Oliver and slapped him with a deafening crack. He cowered even further, nursing his throbbing cheek.

She seethed, pointing a talon between Oliver's eyes, "You don't fuck me, I fuck you."

Stuart Park

# Eight

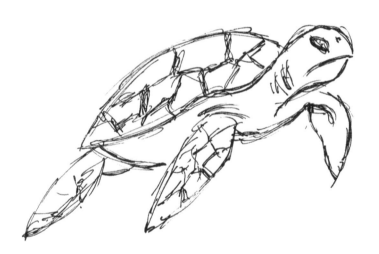

Stuart Park

Mark was aware of a cold throbbing on his right temple as the ringing still persisted. He could hear a man and woman talking over a repetitive muffled beat. Slumped on a sofa he awoke in a small windowless room bathed in a red glow. As he opened his eyes the talking stopped, the muffled beats continued. Kneeling next to him was a smiling girl in her twenties. She pressed a bag of ice to his head.

"Where am I?" Mark slurred.

"Don't worry, you're safe," she reassured him.

"Looks like my brother did a good job on you," pointing to the man across the room.

The brother leapt up, "Sorry, very, very sorry. Gotta go!"

He pushed something into Mark's hand and dashed through a small wooden door. As the door opened the repetitive beats sounded loud and crisp. The door slammed behind him dampening the sounds once more.

Mark sat up and fingered his head.

"It's only a bruise," the girl said softly.

He thanked her and pulled out his phone. Noticing there was no signal he showed the girl a picture of Kate.

"Sorry, you won't find her here."

"Okay," Mark replied, "then I need to go."

The girl pointed to the back of Mark's hand, the swellings had grown.

"Take these," she motioned towards a small bottle on a low table in front of him, the girl had done her research.

"No thanks," Mark refused and stood to leave, clasping his head.

The girl still on her knees raised a hand and wished him good luck.

Her brother had pushed a note into Mark's hand. Mark looked towards the girl and quizzed, "What's this?"

On the small piece of paper was an inked sketch of a swimming turtle.

The girl smiled, "That's also good luck."

Pushing through the door, Mark found himself in a crowded bar with low ceilings. Groups of people huddled around small, randomly spread tables. Neon flickered from the walls illuminating their bottles and glasses. Looking down, the floor was transparent, beneath were shoals of koi carp appearing and disappearing from view, their colour switching with the changing glow. He glanced at a smiling barman staring and pointing to his own head, giving a thumbs-up. Mark smiled back and returned the gesture. The barman waved an empty glass with a quizzical look. Mark shook his head to decline the offer.

He found an exit that led to another windowless room. The music was much louder and was replaced by a single repeating bass drum. Neon covered the walls and ceiling, strobing to the beat, flashing between green, yellow and pink. The gliding fish below his feet now took on an almost illuminous intensity. To one side was a black stone pillar covered with signs that read 'No Dancing'. Looking around this certainly wasn't stopping the local patrons.

In the gloom Mark followed the edge of the room past high sided booths. Some were packed with chatting kids, others with old couples perched on the table in a familiar lotus position, eyes closed and perfectly still. The club seemed to spiral in impossible circles, he lost all sense of direction, and the engulfing waves of dry-ice didn't help. After several minutes of navigating past bouncing revellers and fully mirrored walls, Mark found a nook with an unchanging white glow. As he approached the glimmer, the music changed to a low growl of pure bass, the pitch slowly raised and broke into pulses of industrial brown noise.

The white tinge he'd spotted led to a small dark corridor that zig-zagged into a large circular atrium. The transparent floor led to the centre and erupted into an equally transparent fountain. Several passages exited, acting as a crossroads. Mark watched an old gentleman ushering a lumbering camel into one of the larger openings.

Looking up, jasmine intertwined with a wisteria, branching across the stone walls that seemed to rise for at least five floors. Figures stood on balconies overlooking Mark and the aquatic floor. The ceiling appeared to be glass, he saw stars twinkle in the small patch of clear night sky above. Robed figures sat around the gushing water, dropping in small red pellets, multi-coloured fish breached the surface to feed on these delights. Mark approached one of the younger fish-feeders and showed her the picture, explaining he'd lost his daughter.

"Welcome," beamed the girl, bowing towards Mark.

She offered him some fish-food. Mark dropped some into the water but none of the fish would take his feed. Turning to the phone she studied the picture only to apologise; he knew it was a long shot.

Mark produced the turtle drawing, "So what's this?"

"Ah ha," she exclaimed, pointing towards a far exit. "You need to go that way."

He left the atrium and entered a stone corridor. A doorway on the right led down a set of steps into a darkened room, he was about to pass when he heard a man shouting, "Dog, cat, fishes, turtle." Thinking this might be why the girl sent him this way, he stepped down into the murk. The walls of this low room were covered in a black fibre. The only sources of light were single lamps over each table. Mark shuffled into the den treading carefully so as not to trip. Small groups of people gathered around each table, light chatter tickled his ears. Again he heard the voice, "Dog, cat, fishes, turtle." He turned and headed towards the source.

Behind a table was a squat man with a bulging belly pushing out his maroon waistcoat. Mark pulled up a stool next to a delicate old lady wearing large dark glasses that covered her wrinkled face. She carefully guarded a stack of multi-coloured cash next to a framed photo of two cats, one black and one white; they embraced head-to-tail in a yin-yang configuration.

"Welcome," grinned the portly man, "played 'Bet a Pet' before?"

Mark shook his head.

"It's simple, four cards on the table, you bet, if you win you double your money."

The dealer spread a deck of cards, each card had a sketch of either a dog, cat, turtle or fish. He flipped them all over in one swift movement, the other side showed each card with either a black or green symbol. He pointed to a green symbol. Smiling he said, "Good." Waving a card with a black symbol he frowned saying, "Bad."

"Got it," Mark acknowledged.

Gathering the cards, he shuffled, "Dog, cat, fishes, turtle; thirty-two cards; four good and four bad of each."

He dealt out four cards, they showed a cat, a turtle and two dogs. The old lady counted out a number of notes and placed them on the cat. Mark pulled out his wallet, taking a single note, and laid it on the turtle. The croupier flipped each card, the old lady won on the cat, both the dogs were also green; the turtle showed a black symbol. Mark's money was swiftly removed from the table and sucked into a pneumatic tube. Mark pulled out his phone and showed the dealer an image of Kate, he stared into the middle distance, shrugged his shoulders and bellowed, "Dog, cat, fishes, turtle."

Mark left.

Further along the passage were entrances into other rooms. Approaching one of the doorways he could hear a series of rhythmic deep thuds. Peering inside revealed an elaborate archery range. Men, women and children stood in the vast chamber forming a line stretching as far as Mark could see, all poised in deep concentration.

Mark was hypnotised by the fluid motion of nocking, drawing, aiming and releasing. His eyes followed the liberated projectiles as they disappeared into the distance. He watched as the next arrow was selected without changing their gaze from the target. This repetitive movement reoccurred over and over until all arrows had been fired. Once completed they all burst into large grins and soft chatter. One woman offered Mark her bow, but he politely refused and moved on.

The room opposite brimmed with jet black bonsai trees, pristine white fruit hung from their contorted branches. An elegant lady smiled at Mark but didn't pause as she meticulously harvested the pearl-like berries; wiping each one clean and placing it on a polished granite slab.

The end of the corridor opened into a large area with transparent walls. Mark stood and gasped as ocean creatures drifted past. He approached one wall and watched a manta ray gliding towards the glass, its pectoral fins guided the elegant beast. With one swift movement the fish dived and sunk beneath floor level. A stern looking man produced a small cough, breaking Mark's trance momentarily.

"Sorry sir, Myer is not available."

"Myer?" questioned Mark.

"Yes sir, Myer; not available," the man responded.

"Myer?" questioned Mark, again.

There was a pause.

"Yes sir, Myer; the manta ray," he added. After another pause he continued, "Maybe I can interest you in something else?"

Without noticing, the man had led Mark to a small table adorned with silver knives, forks, spoons and chopsticks. Mark was seated with a napkin laying across his lap. Now paying attention he realised the man was a waiter; looking around, other waiters were ferrying various sized bowls to and from chatting diners.

His waiter pointed towards different walls. "To your right sir I can recommend starting with shallow fried pygmy seahorses and badderlocks. To the right of that, steamed red heart urchin roe; that's to clear the palette of course." The waiter moved to Mark's other side pointing to the left, "If you still have a taste for ray, may I recommend lightly fried Moray eel in Humboldt squid ink with a side of smoked sea cucumber and thongweed, followed by grilled blue jellyfish wrapped in channelled wrack, stuffed in porcupine puffer. A personal favourite I may add." He moved again, "And behind you sir, to finish, baked Bat Sea starfish skewers suspended in Minke whale milk. Simply delightful."

Mark showed his phone to the waiter, "I'm looking for her."

The waiter laughed peering at the girl, "She's not in the tank, but we had one just like her recently. She made such a mess," he tutted.

Mark explained he was looking for his daughter.

The waiter pointed to a stocky man in a private booth, "That's Norton, he's a detective; he could help."

"I don't need a detective," Mark responded with a rare touch of annoyance.

The waiter, oblivious to Mark's tone, suggested the wine list whilst he decided.

Mark removed his napkin and continued through the restaurant. The waiter called out, "Around the corner is our specials wall; take your time."

The room looped, displaying even more of the swimming menu. In one window Mark watched a diver swim into view, netting cuttlefish and scraping limpets from the glass. Further round was the kitchen, Mark could see a white-hatted chef hacking away at a large lump of yellow flesh with what appeared to be a small samurai sword. Next to the kitchen was a battered wooden door, carved into its timber was the image of a turtle.

The stiff door squeaked open, revealing a rusty winding staircase. Mark looked down into the shadows, a breeze of sweet sticky air drifted from below. He checked his phone, still no signal, so decided to head up. After several minutes of climbing the creaking stairs he reached a single metal door, pulling it open he could feel the cool air of the night.

Stepping outside, the door slammed behind him, turning around he noticed there was no handle or lock. The metal exit was featureless apart from the word 'Subanro' etched in the top left corner.

He had appeared at a crossroads, one street was lined with vending machines that disappeared into the darkness. The next was empty, he could see the street dipping down into water, which then disappeared into the distance and the third was full of brightly coloured paper lanterns dancing in the breeze.

Turning to the fourth street he was met by a large reversing lorry using the entire width of the road. A hand grabbed Mark's shoulder and pulled him from the truck's path. The hand belonged to a girl in head-to-toe white leather and a lily white face. A smile revealed she was the same girl he'd met earlier. Over one of her shoulders slumped a body dressed in a blue business suit, which she seemed to carry with ease.

Mark reached for his phone. She stopped his hand without breaking his gaze, "Mister, you should go home, now."

She pointed down the deserted alley of vending machines. Mark simply nodded and followed the narrow road. As he passed the machines, one by one they burst into life making him flinch, readying to defend himself. The canned noodles became illuminated and looked almost appetising; the lights from the machine allowed him to see a little further along the path. A popcorn machine heated up, offering small explosions in a bag. Freshly moulded flowers rotated on a glass platter to the tones of The Blue Danube waltz. A burger machine asked Mark if he was hungry, and sprayed a scent of melted cheese and grilled bacon in his direction, offering him a choice of green or purple relish. Cartoon chickens clucked, asking what sized eggs he needed; each egg sat on an individual set of scales showing their weight.

Each machine was unique and equally bizarre. Mark noted; cupcakes, wine glasses, hens teeth, light bulbs and eunuch beards. Amongst these were donation machines asking to deposit used wigs, rolling pins, underpants and earwax. The lane meandered is some seemingly aimless direction. Turning a corner Mark tripped on a small box and fell, grazing his elbow. A selection of used false teeth scattered across the lane. He guessed there wasn't yet a machine in which to drop these. Climbing to his feet Mark rubbed his head and tended to his bruise, that had already begun to swell. Steadying himself against a wall, he became aware of the familiar sound of a bustling city street.

Turning the next corner, he appeared on a road full of people, noise and confusion. After a pause to let his senses absorb the hubbub, he noticed the shop opposite, 'Kiyoshi Kampo'. In the adjacent alley he could just see his van, still parked where he'd left it.

Mark breathed a sigh of relief.

His phone buzzed with a missed call from Kim. He returned her call "Hey babe, you at home?"

"Yep," Kim responded.

"Is Katie there?" he questioned.

"Yeah, she got back a while ago. I thought she was with you?"

"She was, I've had bit of a crazy day, I'll tell you later," Mark managed to skim over Kate's whereabouts without admitting he'd lost their daughter earlier.

"How crazy can gardening be?" Kim exclaimed with a twinge of irony. "Anyway, not sure what you've done but she stormed in and went straight to her room, slamming all the doors; again. Unless she's still sour from this morning. I'll leave her for you to sort out."

"Well we certainly know she's your kid," Mark smiled knowing he was pushing the boundaries once again. "Okay, it's not too late. I'm going for a swift half," he added before his wife could respond.

"Say *hi* to Sud from me," Kim said knowingly.

# Nine

Stuart Park

"Root Berry," answered a stern voice.

"Yellow Berry," she countered.

"Hello Kimberly, how are you my pretty?" the voice instantly soothed, "You're sounding more husky than usual."

"I need to submit an adjustment," she sobbed.

"This is unlike you, it seems personal. Doesn't sound like a daughter sob, it's a man, but not your husband."

"Moth Berry is compromised," she tried sounding strong.

"I see. I've just had a similar conversation with him. I told you two love birds not to mix business and pleasure."

"How do you—? Never mind," dismissed Kim. "What did he offer you? Just remember how much

Memory Inc. uses your termination services," she continued.

"But this is not a Memory Inc. request; is it now?"

"Don't worry, I can make it stick, what did he offer you?" Kim was worried.

"Listen, Kimberley my dear, I already know the outcome of this conversation. My client's request didn't affect you personally but I'm unable to say more. I am of course bound by client privileges, even though it's not for much longer. But do not worry, it's not about the offer, we're beyond that."

There was a pause to let Kim absorb this.

"I expected your call so suggested that Oliver works late, it gives you time to get home. I'll skip to the chase, how would you like this completed?"

"Not at the office, I was just there," Kim was thinking this through.

"I know, I can hear it on your breath."

"Nothing public, this is not a message. Keep it discrete," she decided.

"Where are the pictures?"

"How—? At his home, in his desk," Kim tried to think what else he might know.

"How about a robbery, a home invasion?"

"Sounds perfect," she agreed.

"I'll look into this matter and treat it with the duty of care you'd expect."

"They are not to look," Kim stated.

"As requested, my people are discrete. We'll retrieve the offending articles and ensure they are safely delivered to you, all part of the service. And Kimberley, you had better find yourself a new therapist."

Stuart Park

# Ten

Stuart Park

A selection of bhangra beats burst into life. Sudheer pulled out his phone, it flashed 'Mild Mark'.

"Yo Slim, what's up?" Sudheer chuckled. "Sure, I was just finishing up anyway," he added. "No, not far, I'm just on the outskirts, in Lythe. We'll give The Green Man a miss after last time. Guess you're not up for Boobs & Bongos?"

Sudheer continued to listen, brushing course, brown hair from his overalls.

"Okay, only a quick one," he confirmed. "The Morning Star it is, see you in a bit."

Mark entered the age beaten pub and made straight for the bar, ordering himself half a lager. The fuzzy TV screen showed a blue team avidly celebrating after beating a red team who were now less than zestful. Taking a sip he wondered if this was knock-off Jaroni from the market. Sudheer was already established in the corner, he had made short work of his pint; foam clung to the inside of the glass defying the vertical drop.

Sudheer studied Mark, "No crisps?"

Mark pulled a packet from his coat, "Brought my own, cheaper that way."

"You little rebel," Sudheer teased. "Anything else in there?"

Depositing his glass, Mark plucked a packet from his other pocket and tossed them across the table.

Sudheer nodded in approval, "Good work my friend, good work. You said you had a bit of a day?" he continued.

Mark told him of the Japanese man not paying.

Sudheer laughed, "Well that's one way to clear your karmic debt."

Sudheer listened to the start of Mark's story, his smile became wider.

"So you were hounded out of your well-earned gravy by a bunch of old crones? That's why you'll always be 'Mild Mark'."

Mark cut in, "Only you call me that, none of my others friends do."

"Sorry mate, you don't have any other friends," he patted Mark on the shoulder.

Mark was about to retaliate, but stopped himself from being pulled further in.

"See," Sudheer twisted the friendly knife with that ear-to-ear grin.

"You only know me because you *had* to sit next to me, it was the only seat left in class," he added. "I'm only messing with you," but Mark knew it was true, that was exactly the non-event that started their friendship.

Mark told his old classmate about the events that followed.

"So you didn't get paid, lost your daughter and ended up in a secret underground city after being bumped on the head."

Mark took a drink.

"You sure you didn't wake up in a bath of ice? Have you checked for stitches?" pointing at his lower back. Sudheer lifted his glass, "And now you're here, sounds like you've had a great day, can it get any better?"

Sudheer took a swig.

"That's enough excitement for one day," Mark sighed.

"Although, I have heard about those leather-clad Japanese punk chicks with that post-modern Geisha look," Sudheer was warming up for a rant.

Mark's friend scanned the pub and leant in, Mark naturally reflected the gesture and tilted forward.

"You've heard of 'The Trust'."

"Sure, everyone knows about The Trust, they probably own this place."

"Right, so I hear," Sudheer looked again. "Apparently these Japanese girls are sent in to *conclude* any business transactions," he used quote-fingers. "Think about it, this Japanese kid turns up in white leather. Whilst you're still scratching your head trying to figure her out, bang! An elbow strike to the Adam's apple followed by a stomp to the side of the knee – or worse – means you can't breathe or run. So now you're on the floor clutching your throat or your balls or both, you're fair game. Now you're thinking, are they the sadistic type? Will this be mercifully quick or are they having a bad day and want to eke it out, savouring every pulled tooth and severed toe? But they don't go for the eyes, no, they want you to see what's coming," Sudheer nodded knowingly.

Mark looked pained.

"If you're really unlucky and they are feeling particularly brutal they'll misalign your chakras and jab you in your third eye – believe me; Kali incarnate," he was on a roll, pausing only for effect. "All that face-paint and lipstick is to hide any scars and scrapes they pick-up on the way. Fact!" Sudheer sat back taking another sip, looking pleased with himself.

"Well *if* that were all true I'm glad I didn't accept his daughter as payment," Mark sounded relieved.

"You what?" exclaimed Sudheer spitting out his drink.

Mark spouted in Pidgin English, "You take my daughter." He added the hip gyration for full effect.

"And you said *no?*" Sudheer spluttered. "You didn't do the needful?"

"Get real, she's barely older than Katie," Mark fought back a grin and pointed a finger towards Sudheer. "Stop … leave it!"

"So, slightly changing the subject, what did Katie get all mad about?"

"I don't know, she hurt her finger, then it was the apocalypse."

"She is certainly Kim's daughter," Sudheer said wittingly.

"That's what I said," agreed Mark.

"Is Kim any better?" probed Sudheer.

"Depends how you define *better*."

"Um, redecorated any walls recently? Or replaced any unusually weak wine glasses? You know, the ones that don't bounce." Sudheer had wondered if he'd gone too far.

"Sorry about that, all I can do is apologise … again," Mark could clearly see the humour in it. "She's taking some tablets and seeing a therapist, all steps in the right direction. Any suggestions from yourself, oh wise guru?"

"I got it, with your skills you could *prune her hysteria!*" he checked for Mark's reaction. This time Sudheer knew he'd pushed the limits too far.

Mark gave a strained grin and changed the subject, "Anyway how's Tammana?"

"She's on fertility leave."

"Need a hand with that?" winked Mark reaching for a crisp.

"It's like a full time job, I have to be back at lunch just to keep the schedule. Look at this."

Sudheer produced a detailed ovulation calendar.

"That's today," Mark pointed out.

Sudheer checked the time, "That's okay, 'Animals in Peril' is on."

Mark looked confused.

"Right now she'll be watching 'save the orphaned polar bears' or some kind of other emotional porn. Bashing the 'pledge here' button whilst wiping away the tears to gawk at more bundles of white fluff being trussed and squashed into cages, then shipped off to some glue factory or fashion designer."

"Not a fan then, huh?" Mark commented. His friend rolled his eyes searching for another crisp.

The TV buzzed to a different channel.

"... beacon in the night's sky, but this place is hell. Its surface temperature is 460°C, that's hot enough to melt zinc. The surface pressure is ninety times greater than that of Earth; some of the first probes sent to Venus only sent back a few images before being crushed into scrap metal. Its skies are covered in storm clouds of sulphuric acid, constantly raining down bolts of lightning. The atmosphere is more than 95% carbon dioxide and its surface is *strewn with volcanoes, that's more than any other plane we know of. This planet is nothing to be celebrated, it is quite literary hell, no wonder it's known as Lucifer. It was the Babylonian goddess Ishtar, worshiped for love and war. Also the Roman goddess of promiscuity and prostitution, and the Mayan god of warfare. This is a bad omen."*

The camera panned from the grey haired naysayer to what appeared to be the host.

*"Thank you reve——"*

"Turn that shit off!" shouted a burly man sat at the bar, "If I wanted a fucking preacher I'd be at home with the wife." The pub gave a ripple of agreement.

The barman obeyed, switching the television to MissileCam LiveTV, then to another game of two teams, this time they were yellow and red. Mark guessed the red team was probably different from the one before. The stocky man mumbled something else before settling back onto his barstool and finishing the dregs of his pint.

"So, what do you think of this Venus thing?" Mark questioned his friend.

"It just means that things in the universe move. One day they're close the next day they're not, everything spins you know, it's all cycles."

Mark pointed to Sudheer's empty glass, "Another one?"

Sudheer checked the time, "Sorry my friend I have ovary duties to attend to."

"Do the needful," smiled Mark as they gathered their things.

Leaving the pub, Mark could hear an unhappy girl playing Manopoly with a cluster of friends huddled around a small table. A band started to setup on a small stage in the far corner. As they left, Mark thanked the bar tender and noticed a poster.

*Battle of the Bands*
*Tonight only*
*The Glow Joes*
*vs*
*Beverly Leaks*

Outside Mark nodded to Sudheer, "Okay, plant-off."

Mark pointed to a tub next to the door.

"Foxtail Amaranth," answered Sudheer with a degree of confidence.

"Okay, too easy I guess. The ones behind it."

Sudheer looked puzzled, "I can't really see in this light."

"Sounds like excuses to me," Mark jabbed as he pulled a crumpled packet of cigarettes from his trouser pocket and offered them.

"Nah thanks, gotta go Stan," Sudheer smirked, walking off towards the car park. "See ya soon, we should check out 'Hooters & Horns'."

"Scarlet Milkweed," shouted Mark as he lit the end of a crooked cigarette.

Sudheer shouted back, "Those things will be the death of you."

Stuart Park

# Eleven

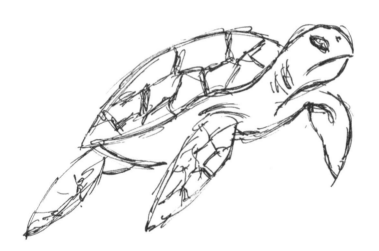

Stuart Park

When Mark arrived home he sensed the house was oddly still. Walking through the lounge he noticed the TV was on. A documentary explained that before the first hydrogen bomb tests, it was unclear if the thermonuclear detonation would ignite all the oxygen and hydrogen in the atmosphere, setting off a chain-reaction around the entire globe. Or simply fuse the desert in New Mexico to glass.

He toed a small vial abandoned on the carpet, it clinked against his boot. On closer inspection the label read 'Kiyoshi Kampo', the rest was hand-scribed in Japanese symbols. The bottle still contained some liquid, he gently sniffed at it but couldn't detect any odour.

Mark called out, "Hello?"

He placed the bottle on a bookshelf next to a family photo, both kids were under ten and he looked much younger.

Approaching the kitchen Mark could hear a rhythmic squelching noise and soft giggling. He could see the floor was strewn in shards of glass and broken crockery. Cutlery and utensils were scattered amongst dented saucepans and fragments of cupboard doors.

Across the room Mark saw a blood-splattered girl clutching his wife's throat, pinning her to the floor. The other hand was clenching a large kitchen knife and stabbing Kim repeatedly in the chest. There was no movement from his wife apart from the jerking of her body as the knife was pulled from her flesh.

"What the …?" Mark gasped, horrified as he took a step towards the girl.

The debris crunched under his feet causing the girl to stop and look up. Under the long matted hair Mark could see the brunette was his daughter. Her entire face and clothes were saturated in blood. She slowly stood, still grasping the blade as crimson liquid dripped from its point making puddles on the tiled floor.

His heart raced.

"Katie?"

She stood facing her dad, her head slightly bowed staring up into her father's eyes. Mark could hear she was breathing heavily, but she didn't answer.

"Honey, put down the knife and tell me what happened," Mark tried not to sound too nervous.

His daughter's eyes shifted to the knife and back to him. She lurched forwards, Mark backed away. Kate reached for a discarded frying pan and launched it at her father. It just missed him as he stumbled back into the lounge. Mark turned to find something to defend himself with, in doing so a broken mug collided with the side of his head. Mark fell to the floor clutching his skull. He flipped onto his back; as he turned, Kate plunged the knife towards his face. Instinctively he raised his hand to protect himself. She drove the blade through his left hand as he screamed in pain. Kate retracted her weapon and thrust again, this time Mark grabbed her arm. He squeezed her wrist forcing her to release the knife and pushed her across the room. He floundered towards the kitchen. His daughter threw a vase which Mark deflected with his arm. Kate swung at her father's head with a wok, this time he was ready and ducked the attack. He knocked the pan from her hand and grabbed the girl who tried clawing at his face. Mark tried to push her away but slipped on the blood and clutter covering the kitchen floor. They both fell. Unable to stop himself, Mark landed on his daughter but his head made contact with the tiled surface.

Blackness.

Mark awoke to a pounding in his right temple and a throbbing from his left hand, followed by a stinging up his left arm. His body ached and the side of his face felt sticky. His vision forced the blurred images into something recognisable. He was still on top of Kate and she was not moving. Mark peeled his face from the floor and lifted himself to his knees. He held his thumping head as his sight fully returned. Looking down he saw Kate's eyes were open as she lay, surrounded in a pool of blood. Something had pierced her neck. It was a crystal stem from a broken wine glass; she must have landed on it as they fell. Mark checked for a pulse, but he already knew it was too late.

"What have I done?" he cried out in anguish.

Scooping up his daughter he cradled her in his arms; tears rolled down his cheeks. As he wiped them away he noticed black marks around the top of her shoulders and neck; that must have been some struggle with Kim.

He could barely raise his head to look over at his wife's lifeless corpse. Picking himself up he shuffled over to Kim's body. Sitting on the floor next to her torso he wept uncontrollably, unable to comprehend the scene in front of him.

He leant his head towards hers, placing a final kiss on her scarlet lips.

Staggering back into the lounge, he sat opposite the droning television holding his head in his hands. The throbbing in his temple dulled but the stinging in his arm had spread into his back and shoulders.

The television vibrated, *"Those who laughed, those who cried and those who were silent felt change breathe upon mankind, the balance was marred and the only morrow be that of demise."*

He stared intently at the grey screen.

*"I have become a gift to the world, that gift be death."*

Mark smiled.

# Twelve

Stuart Park

The black and white grainy images plague his mind.

Mark can feel himself inside a dark storage bay of the Enola Gay, waiting. The doors open and daylight spills in.

At that moment he is set free.

Falling to Earth he feels the rush of air against his face and senses the approaching city below. High above houses and office blocks, burning light consumes all he can see. The instant sun dissolves as quickly as it forms. Consuming firestorms rage across the now razed city. Many thousands are annihilated, becoming mere shadows scorched onto the streets where they once stood. Mark continues to count the dead as searing flesh is replaced by radiation sickness, the creeping destruction reaps all it can find.

An abrupt chiming drew Mark's attention from the television, he scanned the room and became fixated on a wall-mounted clock. The mechanism ratcheted as the tick drifted further from the tock.

Tick.

Mark can see the kitchen. In pure silence he watches the struggle between Kate and his wife. Time slows as Kim loses her footing and falls. Her silent screams for help echo in Mark's mind. He sees his daughter's eyes widen as she reaches for a discarded carving knife from a nearby worktop.

Tock.

Mark feels his daughter drop to her knees and plunge the knife into Kim's chest. He becomes the blade, his arms stretching above his head with sharpened fingers. He feels the air rush past him, holding his breath and sinking below his wife's skin, submerging into the hot crimson liquid.

Tick.

He senses a feeling of contentment, his eyes close and he drifts with unbounding pleasure. He is only aware of this perfect moment, nothing else exists except sheer absolution.

Tock.

Kate withdraws the knife and he releases his breath. He watches small specks of red trail down the gleaming white fridge. He begins to pant in frustration, eager to return into the soft folds.

Tick.

The knife plummets. This time Mark's fingers strike a rib bone, a chipped fragment skids across the floor and rests amongst the carnage. Another swing finds himself immersed in pure bliss. His fingers pierce Kim's lung. He grabs at the torn tissue and allows the blood to fill the empty void.

Tock.

The television flashed and groaned as the room returned. He clamped his teeth and stifled a cry from the stinging that wracked his body.

Mark staggered back to the kitchen. Stepping over his dead family, he ran the cold tap and doused his head. He watched the red water trickle from his chin and spiral into the abyss below.

Sally smooths out the blanket as she unpacks the carefully prepared picnic. Through her sunglasses she watches Finn paddle in the shallows of the lake, rubbing off excess sun cream. She settles with a book, adjusting her hat to shade the pages. Her son feels brave, spying a fish he wades further from the shore. Once Finn can no longer feel the bottom he breaks into a crude doggy-paddle.

"Hey mum, I'm swimming!" he shouts.

"Just be careful," his mother calls in reply.

The boy spots a small island and heads towards it. Below the surface Mark's eyes open as he hears the muffled sounds from above. He unfurls and stretches towards the splashing boy. Finn can feel a tightness around his ankle and begins to kick at the water. He waves his arms in desperation and screams for his mother. Looking up she can see her son panicking and clasping for invisible handholds. She rushes to the water's edge and shrieks his name. The boy cannot break Mark's grip as he is slowly pulled under. Finn looks up to see the bright ripples slowly fade from his reach and stares down to the murky depths. His lungs start to burn and his pulse quickens as confusion sets in. When he can no longer hold on, he breathes.

The lake fills his mouth and windpipe, his throat convulses and body writhes struggling to expel the water. As blackness fills his vision he glances up one last time to see his terrified mother frantically clawing at the surface. Once devoid of oxygen, Mark releases the boy and watches as he floats freely in the gloom, being taken at the lake's whim.


Clearing his eyes with the palms of his hands he surveyed the scene. Mark worked to regain control of his mind and to figure out how this happened. Maybe he could retrace his steps, the shop in Hanro, the market, the rickshaw driver, the underworld. As the stinging skewered his spine he was overcome by one simple urge, the desire to destroy.

Driving through the city he hungered to swerve into pedestrians, he fought the steering wheel as if battling an invisible force. He hit curbs and refuse sacks; other drivers sounded their horns and flashed their lights. A couple crossing the street dived from Mark's path as he accelerated towards them. By the time Mark reached Mr Kiyoshi's shop his heart was pumping and he was drenched in sweat. He fell from the van and desperately avoided eye contact with the evening's revellers. A string of red light bulbs hummed overhead as he started to drift ...

Mark stands in a brightly lit room, the once white paint was chipped, and yellowed with age. In front of him is a large iron lever with a red handle, behind him is a sunken mirror spanning the wall's entire width. To one side a masked figure struggles against the straps, but is held firm. He can hear the muffled pleas from beneath the hood and can see the writhing body is bound to a dense wooden—

"You okay?" shouted a voice over the background dim.

Mark drifted back. He could see a figure smoking in the alley, dressed in black and white chequered trousers and an apron. He pointed towards Mark. The stinging surged as rage took control. He stumbled towards the man, picking up a length of wood.

"What's up buddy?" questioned the chef. "What are you doing?"

Mark raised the makeshift club above his head. Bringing down his weapon the man leapt back.

"You crazy, wha—," was all he could manage as Mark took another swing, this time hitting him to the ground. Before Mark could make another attempt the cook was on his feet and the wood was knocked from his hand.

"Get outta here," demanded the man pointing back to the street.

Mark ignored the warning and lunged towards him. His momentum was redirected face-first into the wall. He collapsed like a rag doll.

Regaining his balance he charged. His attack was cut short by a side-kick to Mark's stomach with a leather clog. The defender now had Mark on the ground pinning his head under his patterned knee, preparing for a punch.

"Stop!" shouted an appeal from behind them, "he's a friend." Kiko stepped from the shadows.

"How long you been there?" queried the chef.

"Long enough," smiled Kiko.

"He's not so friendly," the man disagreed, releasing Mark.

"Hey mister!" snapped the girl, "you should have gone home sooner."

Mark groaned but remained still.

Kiko laughed, "Ah well, I was going out, but this will be much more fun."

# Thirteen

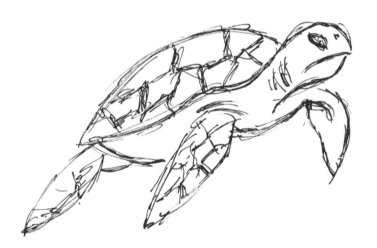

Stuart Park

Kiko hoisted a beaten Mark over her shoulder and carried him into the shop and up the stairs. She placed him on her bedroom floor and studied his dazed state.

"You've been having some fun," she muttered at him.

Crouching down, she began to pick fragments of glass from his temple and cheek. She washed the dried blood from his left hand and wrapped it in gauze.

Mark realised he was no longer in a dark alley. He was slumped on a wooden floor amongst a vibrant collection of discarded wigs. The room was highly decorative, lit by red candles randomly placed wherever space allowed. Some candles were seated in floor-standing holders, others were amongst books, carved wooden boxes and bottles of varying colour liquids. Black smoke from the candles drifted effortlessly towards the stained ceiling where ivy crept across the crumbling plaster. The walls were adorned with red and black fabric depicting fierce dragons and snarling tigers. Next to this hung parchment covered in hand-painted Japanese symbols and detailed sketches of maple blossom.

He could see the Japanese girl sat at a small desk, grinding away with a pestle and mortar, adding in a brown viscous oil and grinding again. She was dressed in the familiar white leather and still had the painted face to match. Mark felt the stinging contort his body as his arms spasmed and neck twitched.

Kiko looked over, "Glad you're still with us. I think you need some advice on who *not* to pick a fight with. He maybe a chef, but my advice is, not with him."

Mark peered up at her.

"This is for your cuts," she nodded at the small bowl in her palm. "And that is for those stings on your hand," turning her gaze towards a small brown vial. "You didn't take payment from my father, in my eyes we still owe you."

Mark picked himself from the floor, wiping blood from his eye. Arms outstretched, he launched himself at the girl. She stood and dodged his attack with ease, guiding him towards one of her many mirrors. Collapsing to the floor, Mark had a new wound on his forehead, now garnished with more glass.

"You are lots of fun mister," Kiko giggled.

She approached him still laughing. Although seated, Mark swung at her. She swatted away his punches with little effort. Whilst evading his attempted strikes, the girl picked the new pieces of glass from his head.

"Well if you won't keep still …" she lifted the man, depositing him on her bed.

Before Mark could attempt another attack, Kiko had bound his wrists and ankles with leather bonds securely fastened to each bed post. Mark strained at the shackles, his body surging with agony. Kiko calmly plucked smaller fragments of glass from his temple. She leant over the man and kissed his fresh wound, licking her lips. Mark could see some of her porcelain white face was splattered with his blood. He writhed on the bed, pulling at the straps. It was clear his agony aroused Kiko.

He watched as she slowly unzipped her skin-tight, ivory leather one-piece and peeled it from her torso. As she uncovered, Mark could see her entire figure was painted white. Her small pert breasts and perfect form stepped closer to the bed. The girl ripped open Mark's shirt and traced a single fingernail across his chest to his waist. She plucked a candle from a bedpost and dripped hot wax onto his body, following her already drawn path. The girl loosened Mark's belt and exposed his penis. Licking the inside of his thigh with the tip of her tongue meant he was now completely erect.

Kiko straddled her hostage running her clitoris up and down his stiff shaft, she gave a soft moan as she lubricated them both. Lifting herself, she slowly positioned her vagina to nudge the end of Mark's member. In small circles she gradually opened herself and began to envelop Mark. She bit her lip and fully consumed him, tensing her pelvic muscles she watched the wrath in his eyes grow. He followed her white breasts rising and falling with each controlled thrust as her breathing became deeper. Mark tried to reach for the girl but the bonds held fast, only enraging him further. She impaled herself further with each forceful sway to find the deepest point. Not quite finding it she repositioned herself to face away from her captive, grinding down on Mark to gain that perfect spot. Her hips moved in wider circles, squeezing Mark with every revolution. Kiko raised her hands above her head and clasped them together as if in prayer. Mark could see two snakes drawn on her enamel back, they followed the curves of her waist, mapping the contours of her figure. She clutched him and held perfectly still to stop him releasing too soon. Turning again to face Mark she swiped a blonde wig from the floor. The golden strands tumbled down her shoulders as she increased the strength of her strokes. She screamed, "Fuck me daddy!" Knowing he could no longer resist. The girl shifted and started to massage the mushroom end of Mark's penis with her moist lips. Mark felt the tension rise to breaking-point and could restrain himself no more. One last squeeze from Kiko and he erupted inside her. He could feel himself throbbing, pressing against the walls of her vulva. She gripped him once more, sucking out every last drop he had to offer.

A calmness descended over Mark as the stinging subsided; he at last felt some ease. His attention was drawn from the ivory girl to the pale light in the night sky.

In this glow Kiko emits a silvery aura reflecting in all the candles and glass bottles. This becomes intensely bright and makes Mark squint. He watches a moth fly in through the open window and lifts his head to track its meandering path. Without any sign of apprehension it flies into the flame of a free-standing candle. The moth ignites and its ashes dissipate in the breeze. Another moth enters through the window and befalls the same crematory fate. This is followed by another and another, the room is filling with the beating of tiny wings taking turns to extinguish their existence without any precursor of anxiety or judgement.

Mark tries to sit up and watch the annihilation light show, he pulls at his restraints; this time they give way. Looking up at Kaylyn he can feel himself still inside her as he grabs for her neck. She clutches his wrists but is powerless to break his grip. His hands tighten as she attempts to scream but is unable to make a noise. After she fights, beating at Mark's hands, her body convulses and eyes bulge. Finally she goes limp.

He releases her and she slumps to his chest. He can feel himself stir again—

Fingernails dug into Mark's chest and raked down his torso. Pulling at his arms, he realised he was still trapped as the stinging sensation amplified.

"Going somewhere mister?" she jested. "Okay, but be good."

She unleashed him, keeping one hand firmly on his chin. Once freed she slowly withdrew her grasp.

Before he could move, Kiko flipped Mark onto his front. She ripped off his shirt and dug her nails into his shoulders, this time drawing blood. The stinging intensified as he tried to buck, but she had him pinned. Kiko noticed a large marbled effect tattooed across Mark's left arm and back.

"Didn't think you were the type," she stated approvingly.

The girl traced the markings with a bloody finger, matching the swirls and loops as they spiralled and drifted in irregular patterns. Kiko paused, doubting her eyes. It must had been the flickering from the candles. She drew nearer, no she was right, the tattoo was creeping across Mark's body. She gasped and flinched in horror, flipping Mark on his back she bound his wrists and watched as black ringlets worked their way over his shoulder and onto his chest. Mark wailed and pulled at his bonds. He studied his chest, following where Kiko was pointing; terror filled her green eyes.

"Nani Kore … Yokai Nara!" she screeched.

"What the, get it off!" fear saturated his mind.

Wiping the blood from her finger she spied a black speck slowly increasing in size. Dashing to a drawer in a nearby cabinet she pulled out a long wooden box holding three syringes. With one swift motion Kiko plunged the long needle of the syringe into her left thigh. Her pupils dilated and heart began to pound even before the syringe was removed.

"What are you doing?" he commanded.

"Adrenalin, plus my own special concoction," she squirmed, pulling the needle from her thigh.

Rushing back to the bed she reached under the mattress and pulled out a long bladed knife. Placing her index finger on the bedpost, in one swift motion she swung at the tip of her digit. In a single slice the end was severed, it rolled off the bedstead and bounced as it hit the wooden floor.

Kiko pointed to Mark with her bleeding stump, "That … you need to get it off."

Mark's chest was covered in black whirlpools. He snarled at her as his wrists bled from the constant pulling of his restraints.

The girl reached for another loaded syringe and sunk it into Mark's thigh. He could see the clear liquid was whirling with green smoke. She released his hands as the fluid pulsed through his body, his eyes widened and his heart beat faster than he could imagine; clarity edged through the fog.

Mark fell to his knees, clutching his ears as the deafening pounding from his heart echoed around his skull. He could feel the stubble on his chin edging its way through his follicles and could taste the struck-match aroma of sulphur dioxide from a volcano on a distant continent. Beetles scraped at the underside of the wooden floorboards and a spiders' eyes twitched in the direction of new prey in its web.

"You know what this is?" Mark demanded.

"Yokai Nara, it's an old legend, some kind of ancient demon, it *will* consume you," she panicked, backing away.

The blackness had inched its way from Mark's back, creeping over his left shoulder to his chest, as it picked up momentum. His mind became crystal clear.

He looked at Kiko still holding the knife, "May I?"

She handed him the blade.

Taking a deep breath he stared at the knife now in his right hand. He jabbed the silver tip into his left shoulder and began to slice around his nipple, over his ribcage and down to his stomach. Kiko looked on in amazement as blood leaked from his incision, pooling on the floor.

Mark breathed again, anchoring himself on the bedpost, and through gritted teeth he started again from his left shoulder. He worked the knife across his collar bone, down the right side of his chest and back to his stomach, creating a large red circle on his torso.

Starting from the top he used the blade to peel the skin away from his body, from his shoulders to his waist. He worked his way down with each cut, exposing bone and muscle with every slice. Mark watched the flaps of skin slump to the floor, he kept carving until his upper body was a mass of tendons and sinews.

He stepped back with a giant grin admiring his grisly achievement, sweat dripping from his victorious face. He looked at Kiko who was pointing at his waistline, he dropped his trousers and realised he'd not done enough. The blackness had crept down his right thigh and across his groin. Lifting his coal coloured penis, he gaped at his equally covered scrotum. Mark looked at the knife in his hand.

*Fuck that!*

Tossing the knife to one side he zipped his fly and grabbed the wooden box from the cabinet, now containing a single primed syringe. Mark gathered up his slippery flesh and headed towards the door.

Kiko called out, "Hey, you missed a bit".

Scooping up his forgotten skin, Mark pointed to the girl, "Hey, so have you."

Stuart Park

# Fourteen

Stuart Park

Mark staggered back down the dimly lit stairs, exiting into the alley.

A circle of loitering teenagers were outside sharing stories and passing round a large spliff. They watched as a door slammed and a man darted towards the road.

One of the youths shouted, "Hey, have you seen Ki—"

He stopped mid flow as the half-naked man sprinted past, clutching an armful of bloody skin that should have been attached to his body.

Mark looked over, "I really wouldn't."

Mark knew these kids had been ripped off. He could smell the Moroccan honey they were smoking consisted of only four percent THC, the rest was made up from milk powder, ground coffee and dark tan boot polish. The lad shouting hadn't been smoking long, the Yellow

Twig tobacco would make his head spin more than the substandard hemp he mixed with it.

Taking a drag and shrugging his shoulders the boy shouted, "Why?"

This time Mark didn't answer, although on the wall behind them he noticed Black Spleenwort.

His van was still where he'd abandoned it earlier. The teenagers stared as Mark threw the skin on the passenger seat of his vehicle, exposing his peeled chest. He climbed in the driver side, clicked in his seatbelt and started the engine, kicking the radio into life. The presenter was interviewing Venus gazers, commenting on how the planet was almost at its fullest and brightest in the sky. Mark scratched the lumps on the back of his hand, yellow puss oozed down his arm. He wiped the sweat from his brow and quashed the radio; he needed to concentrate.

He reversed back into the road narrowly missing two guys in platinum blonde wigs. One was wearing a silver latex cat suit and frosted platforms, the other had violet PVC leggings and a rose chiffon scarf with matching bittersweet stilettos. They squealed as the gardener's van lurched across the pavement. Taking one look at Mark, they teetered and recalled their protest.

The turtle bobbed.

The night had come alive, Hanro was bustling with noise and activity.

Tables had appeared outside restaurants, restless diners feasted on cibreo marinated in merlot served with rigatoni and fresh basil. Khash and Tong Zi Dan eggs seemed a popular choice; Mark could taste the still steaming ammonia as it was served. Fast food patrons snacked on Rocky Mountain Oysters and imported cicada. Taverns served up bar snacks of jing leed and jumiles with dipping salsa. A special at The Meat Grinder offered Venus Vesper suggesting it was the classic Vesper flavoured with voavanga and vanilla. This certainly wasn't Madagascar Bourbon, the hint of butterscotch suggested it was Jeffrey Pine resin instead. Other modest clientele finished their evenings early with a black ivory coffee complemented with smoked mesquite and lemongrass chocolate.

Clutching his head, the flavours and aromas that Mark absorbed overwhelmed his senses.

He could hear two chefs chatting in hushed tones as they prepared a tiger blowfish for an arms dealer to impress his potential client.

"I'm not sure I'm getting this, you're taking coke every day."

"Well, coke and speed; but yes, every day."

"You take it to stay awake, right?"

"Yeah, it's so I can keep going through these fourteen hour shifts."

"Do you ever sleep?"

"Um, not much."

"But, how can you afford it?"

"Easy, I work these long shifts."

Orange street lamps mixed with royal blue and lime green strobed from the bar opposite, emitting an eerie glow. Mark looked down, his crimson chest changed colour in the flickering lights. He could feel the effects of Kiko's unique adrenalin blend wearing off and the pain seeping in to fill its place. With it he could sense the familiar stinging and urge to kill. He needed to head away from populated areas, out of town, somewhere he could do less damage.

As Mark pulled away, the dulling of his awareness was a welcome relief but the rising strain in his limbs was not. He gripped the wheel and focussed on retaining control, his chest throbbed with each heartbeat.

His eyes darted from the speedometer to the drunken party goers and back again. He watched a parade of goth girls in top hats and corsets pick their way through tattooed Muscle-Mary's having a flex-off, whilst college kids in Hawaiian shorts and Ray-Ban's looked for the nearest party.

The side of a four storey building was being used as a projection screen showing Eraserhead. The black and white images flickered in shop windows as a giant Jack Nance peered down on the viewers below.

Mark could feel his grasp slipping away, he began to accelerate trying to leave the city behind him.

Colossal lanterns hung over the road between the buildings. They swayed in the night's breeze like gargantuan jellyfish drifting in an ocean current. Mounds of day-glow rubbish formed the backdrop for two magicians spinning plates and juggling burning torches. Youngsters wearing thick wooden masks and draped in unkempt animal fur chased each other through the magician's makeshift stage, trying to tip the revolving plates from their sticks. Cages of mewing Siamese cats were stacked at the mouth of an alley, some of the hungry animals were poised, watching the free roaming chickens peck at grey chewing gum trodden into the street. Two ornate women in purple and gold bartered over a caged, white kitten. The attached shop advertised turtle shell ashtrays and woolly mammoth rugs.

Mark began to leave the neon lights and commotion behind. He passed huge graffiti covered advertisements for Nova Space Tours; the letters 'va' had been sprayed out. The 'See You Soon' slogan called to him like an unknown messenger.

The stinging had become more intense. Mark struggled to keep the vehicle straight. He had an impulse to swerve into oncoming traffic. He shouted, screamed and fought with himself but his resistance weakened.

Mark stared at a tree rooted next to a street lamp. He recognised the familiar leaves and the way the tips of its branches swayed, but could not recall its name.

He felt himself letting go, slowly succumbing to the growing wrath. Ahead he could see a petrol station, several cars and a lorry were filling up. He accelerated towards the nearest customer using a pump. At the last moment he sounded his horn to alert his unsuspecting target. Hearing the warning, his prey launched himself away from the speeding van as Mark collided into the pump and a green Audi.

The ladders catapulted from the top of Mark's vehicle, the momentum breaking them free of their straps. The man sprinted away from the scene but could not outrun the velocity of the flying metal. He was impaled through the back of his head, the aluminium embedding itself in his skull. One end of the ladder was still attached to the roof of Mark's van. On the other end dangled the man, his arms and legs hanging limp akin to some grisly, suited puppet.

# Fifteen

Stuart Park

The swinging turtle's head was the first thing Mark noticed as his vision returned; other smudges of colour and texture gradually became recognisable shapes. The pain also snapped back, the stinging now consumed his entire body. The impact had jolted the driver's side wing mirror. He could see himself.

He sat and watched the black smoke drift over his face, his arms and hands, swirling with dark patterns. Mark turned the key in the ignition but the engine failed to respond. The driver's side door was crumpled shut. He unbuckled his seatbelt and pushed himself to the passenger side.

He needed to get out, he needed to kill.

Mark crawled out, collecting up his skin. In amongst the flesh and gore was Kiko's hand-carved wooden box; flipping open the lid was the final syringe nestled in waves of white silk. The needle had snapped in half leaving a jagged end, but the green mist in its barrel rolled in the clear liquid. Laying on the forecourt he heard the sound of running liquid, he saw the collision with the pump had ruptured the feed and the fuel was edging its way towards him. Looking up, an attendant was running his way.

Mark got to his feet and growled, "Go away!"

Grasping the van door, he fought the urge to chase the young man down and squeeze the life from his body.

The teenager took one look at the spreading petrol and Mark's skinned body. He called, "I'll get help," and ran back to the shop.

Mark scooped up the syringe but his body resisted. In an act of rebellion against himself, he thrust the barbed needle into his shoulder. He fell backwards as the world crashed in on him.

There were six heartbeats in the service station shop, two were smokers and one of those was likely to die from emphysema within the next eight months; that was, if they lived past tonight. They all stared at Mark intently.

One corner of the roof over the pumps housed a nest of a few hundred European hornets, their incessant buzzing vibrated through Mark's head. This was matched only by the unrelenting drone of the flood lights; the pulsating tungsten etched into his brain.

Mark caught the stench of the decaying prawn mayonnaise sandwich that was lodged behind the chiller cabinet in the shop, it hadn't been there long, but in another four days everyone would know. Magma roared beneath his feet, desperately seeking fissures in the crust to free itself, and a dandelion grew.

Getting to his feet he realised he was paddling in fuel from the pump; but not enough.

He grabbed the abandoned pump from the floor, the one his victim had been using. He held it over his head and squeezed the trigger. Looking up he noticed only a few drops falling from the end of the nozzle. Glancing towards the shop he saw the attendant had hit the emergency 'pump off' safety switch. Opposite Mark's vehicle sat the lorry, its driver had since fled. Dashing to the back of his van he grabbed his father's trusty axe, it had seen better days but for now it would serve its purpose.

Sirens sounded in the distance, he could taste the driver's bad breath, the mint he sucked on certainly didn't help. Mark clutched at his chest, his hummingbird heart felt as if it would explode at any instant.

The forecourt was clear.

Mark grasped the axe handle and hacked away at the exposed fuel tank of the lorry until the metal dented with the force. After several attempts he forged a crack and the diesel hissed from the fracture.

Gathering his skin, he dumped it on the now sodden ground. He reached into his pocket for his crumpled cigarettes placing one between his lips. From his other pocket he pulled out his phone, flicking through the contacts he found 'Sudheer' and smiled.

"Hey Mark, it's late, what's up buddy?" he sounded tired.

"Listen my friend …" started Mark, "a squirrel named Larry worked hard finding and burying an abundance of acorns during the autumn. A squirrel named Susie frolicked around in the autumn but didn't make any provisions for the winter. As the seasons changed Larry sought out his food stash, but little did he know a crow had watched him hide his rations."

Sudheer tried to interrupt. Mark kept talking.

"The crow helped himself to the secret supply. Larry saw the crow steal his reserves and watched Susie become very hungry. Larry convinced Susie to bargain with a starving cat; he would share his acorns with Susie if she persuaded the cat to dispatch the crow. Susie told the cat where to find a plump crow and a well-fed squirrel. The cat was happy for the meal. It killed the crow and later hunted down Larry."

"What are y—," Sudheer attempted.

Mark didn't stop, "The cat waited until Susie fleshed out whilst feasting on Larry's hoard; the cat then dined on Susie. An uneaten acorn remained buried until the spring where it started to grow. After several weeks the sapling began to branch and leaves sprang from new buds, this was later devoured by a passing deer."

After a pause he heard Sudheer begin to speak again, Mark said nothing more. As painful as it was, he silenced his friend. Nothing more could be said.

Still staring at his phone, tears started to build in Mark's eyes, he knew there was something he must do. He jabbed at the screen, forging a new message. Through his bleary gaze he read it back and hit send. He couldn't bear to speak. Mark felt the vibrations in the air and returned the phone to his pocket.

He could hear Kiko whisper, "Don't do it, there is another way."

Mark sparked his lighter into life, he could feel Kiko's adrenalin mixture losing its potency as the familiar sting claimed his muscles. He focussed on the flame, watching it twitch in the breeze. Creating gun-fingers he raised them to his head and peered towards the onlookers in the shop.

"There is no other way," breathed Kaylyn.

Mark lit the right-angled cigarette.

The approaching fire crew could see a ball of flame in the inferno of the petrol station's forecourt. Black fumes bellowed from the burning mass, once past the halogen flood lights the thick smoke disappeared into the blackness of the night. Above the city a flock of sky lanterns drifted in the currents, amongst them Venus shone bright, the galactic metronome ticked on as she cast an eye over her sister. With the planetary conjunction now complete, the galactic pentagram was fully consummated.

Hesperus was now home to yet another fallen angel.

# Epilogue

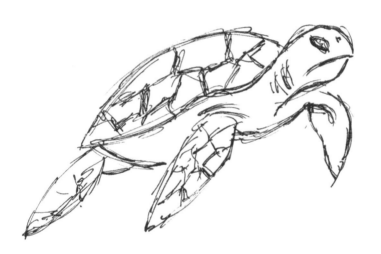

Stuart Park

"Get some sleep," Lucy ordered with a smile.

Ben nodded and returned with a similar grin.

He entered the locker room and lowered himself onto a bench.

"What a day," he sighed.

It had been a long shift that felt more drawn-out than usual. He'd seen more assaults and knife wounds today than he would on any Saturday night.

He closed his eyes and sunk his face into his palms. The darkness carried a comfort, memories of warmth from before he could remember, or maybe a forgotten dream. He was not alone, she'd keep him safe, somehow he just knew, without words he felt it to be true. Ben knew but he reached out all the same, he stretched in all directions desperate to know it was true. Despite his efforts and belief, no one was there. She was never there.

The door opened. A voice broke Ben's spell, "Long day, huh bud?"

"You know it," Ben rubbed his eyes and rolled his neck.

Changing from his loose fitting scrubs, he searched his pockets for some change and feasted on a chocolate bar from a nearby vending machine. He couldn't remember the last time he'd consumed anything. He should have accepted that coffee from his sister this morning.

Leaving the hospital, he wished good night to his fellow colleagues in A&E. Stood at the entrance he pulled up his collar to protect himself from the rain. Getting the keys ready he dashed to his car, avoiding puddles and small streams. Raindrops drummed on his roof as he squeezed the water from his dark hair. He shuddered as it dripped onto his neck and rolled down his back. Taking a breath, Ben checked his phone. A couple of text messages, one from dad, that's odd.

*Don't go home, find the girl at kiyoshi kampo, love you, sorry, dad*

Ben tried calling his father but was transferred straight to voice mail.

> *Hi, um, thanks for calling, this is Mark Goode,*
> *please leave me a message and I'll get back to you*
> *when I can.*

He tried to call the house, but again there was no answer, so he decided to head for home, ignoring his father's warning.

The city was busy for this hour of the morning, especially in this weather. He passed workmen in orange overalls carrying lengths of blue piping. There were scores of burnt out paper lanterns scattered across pavements and shop awnings, their smouldering remains sizzling from street lights and telephone poles.

Ben clicked on the radio to stay awake. Ah yes, it was the Venus thing earlier this evening, not to happen again for another 3,000 years. Typical, once in a lifetime event and he missed it. Ben looked up at the sky, it was pure black, now there was no chance of seeing anything with all this cloud cover.

Wipers squeaked across his windscreen.

The local news told of an explosion at a petrol station on the outskirts of town.

> *"The police have yet to issue a full statement,*
> *current speculation is a small scale terrorist attack*
> *or a drone misfire. Two bodies were at the scene.*

*The family of the first victim has been notified. The second body has yet to be identified."*

Ben arrived home. Before he could climb from the car a neighbour rushed out in bare feet to meet him. A scrawny man introduced himself as Jerry; he shielded his face from the rain with a half-eaten doughnut. He told Ben he'd heard crashing noises and shouting a few hours ago but since then it had all been quiet. He would have called the police but didn't want to make a fuss.

Ben thanked him whilst trying to determine the different stains on this man's faded t-shirt. Jerry nodded and padded back home through the puddles. Ben could see a sizable woman waiting at the neighbour's door. She called to Jerry saying she was hungry; he squawked, telling Doreen to get back inside before anyone saw.

Ben could see his mother's car in the drive, but the van was nowhere. He entered the house and stepped into the lounge calling out to anyone that might answer. The television was on and the answer machine flashed with four unheard messages. The room had been wrecked, he called again, still nothing. He crept into the kitchen to see his mother and sister lying in pools of blood. He stumbled backwards falling to the floor in disbelief; his heart raced as he gasped for breath. Ben picked himself up and slowly approached Kate, broken glass crunched under his feet. He should be used to this, his days are spent looking at beaten and broken bodies, but not like this, not his own family.

Instinctively he crouched down, taking a big gulp, he checked for a pulse in her neck; nothing. Her face was ashen, but Ben noticed unusual black marks around the top of her neck and shoulders. Standing again he turned to his mother. His stomach felt tight, there was a lump in his throat he just couldn't swallow. Kneeling by her side he could see her torso had been mutilated, the thick ruby liquid had begun to harden. Again, he checked her pulse, but he knew it was too late; her cool skin already looked purple and waxy.

He could no longer hold back the emotions. He screamed in anger as tears flooded down his cheeks, dripping from his chin. He was lost, his whole world had crumbled before him. More than ever he reached out but no one was there to pull him close. She wasn't there.

Ben was startled as the house phone started to ring. Could this be dad?

He gathered himself and picked his way into the lounge. It was not his father, it was Sudheer saying he had a strange call from Mark. Something about squirrels and acorns and crows and hungry cats. He said he understood it, but it was unlike his dad. Since then he couldn't reach his mobile and this was the first time someone had answered the home phone. He asked if everything was alright. Ben said he couldn't talk right now. Sudheer offered his help if anything was wrong. Ben kept it together and thanked Sudheer, saying this was not a good time.

Heading back into the kitchen Ben saw the familiar family photo laying smashed on the carpet, he picked it up and stifled a sob. Next to the picture was a small bottle of liquid he'd never seen. The label read Kiyoshi Kampo, he recognised that from his dad's message. Wiping his eyes he checked for the address, pausing to hear a clap of thunder. Ben realised this place was in Hanro, which was not far.

Maybe it was time to find that girl.

# ABOUT THE AUTHOR

Stuart is not an author.

Then something happened.
Following a knee operation he found himself
incapacitated for a spell. Overnight he was immobile and
learnt a keen lesson in loss. This new sense of frustration
didn't sit well with him. Reviewing his then limited
options he decided to vent by writing. Writing had always
been on his bucket list and this seemed to be the perfect
opportunity.

Stuart tells himself he's not an author. This belief is what
makes him not an author.

He has helped out the Sinister Horror Company by
proofreading titles, including: Terror Byte, Punch, Class
Three, Upon Waking, Class Four and Hexagram for JR
Park and Duncan P Bradshaw.
He also has a keen interest in photography and produced
an abstract photography book called 'Escapee'. Some of
his work can been found here:
LikeBreathing.com

Remember, Stuart is not an author. At least that's what
he believes, so it must be true.

# MARKED: POP QUIZ

1) What does 'buinasu, aishiteru' mean?

2) What is 'C11 H17 N3 O8' and where would you find it?

3) What did Mark slip on in the market?

4) Why wouldn't the fish take the feed from Mark?

5) Why does Sudheer call Mark 'Slim' and 'Stan'?

6) Who or what was 'Enola Gay'?

7) What is Venus' sister planet?

8) If Oliver changed his car tyres would it be the same car?

9) What is a common name for 'Foxtail Amaranth'?

10) Who is the 'suited puppet'?

Stuart's short story *Oranges Are Orange* is featured in the charity anthology The Black Room Manuscripts Volume Two by the Sinister Horror Company.

Alzheimer's Research UK — The Power to Defeat Dementia

All profits from the sale of the anthology will go to Alzheimer's Research UK.

SinisterHorrorCompany.com

Facebook.com/SinisterHorrorCompany

Twitter @SinisterHC

Lightning Source UK Ltd.
Milton Keynes UK
UKOW06f1914080816
280250UK00015B/218/P